Queen of Hearts

ALICE LA ROUX

Author's Note

This is a mafia romance centered around a gang I have created in a fictional town. This may surprise you, but I have never been in the mafia, and I have never murdered anyone so bear that in mind. This book is a work of fiction about a female badass and the man who supports her, so please enjoy it for what it is.

I've categorized it as dark because Rosie can be a little bloodthirsty, but I know for many of you, it won't be dark enough. Sorry about that, but this book kind of wrote itself and this is how it turned out. I hope the snark and sexy times between Rosie and Jay make up for it.

Violence, sexual situations, drugs, gangs, childhood abuse, weapons, homicide, arson are all mentioned, some in more detail and graphic than others.

Playlist

Nothing More – Go To War

Moncrieff x Judge – Serial Killer

Klergy & Valerie Broussard – Start A War

Grandson – Despicable

Lola Blanc – Angry

June – A Little Messed Up

Halsey – Control

Sigrid – Everybody Knows

K/DA – Villain ft. Madison Beer & Kim Petras

KiNG MALA – Cult Leader

Stella Jang – Villain

Rezz – Taste of You ft. Dove Cameron

For those who like to read about ants...
Those who know, know.

*"...if you drink much from a bottle marked "poison,"
it is almost certain to disagree with you, sooner or later."*
— Lewis Carroll, Alice in Wonderland

Welcome to

WunderLnd

Prologue

Rosie

T've always liked to play with fire, and that's why I refused to live on the side-lines of my father's world. I embraced the darkness he invited into our lives, watching, waiting, learning the tricks of the trade, all while getting my nails manicured and pretending publicly that I was just another Family daughter. After all, Family daughters were pampered princesses, coddled by our men, wrapped up safely in silk and jewels. Put on display like trophies. Good wives and good daughters were markers of great men, a reflection on how powerful and capable they were. My father however understood that sometimes a beautiful face was also a liability, and he encouraged my extra-curricular interests. In fact, it was him who bought me my first firearm. From there my interests grew, as I imagined not needing a man the way my mother did my father. I wanted to be more than a decorative ornament, bartered for power and used for leverage. I wanted more. My father secretly approved, my mother not so much but the patriarch ruled in our household: his word was law.

I saw my first dead body when I was eight and killed my first traitor when I was thirteen. I still remember how it felt to cut into the man's flesh like I was carving into raw meat, my knife sliding in, crimson blossoming against the pale tones of his skin. Even if his face has faded over the years, his screams still echo in my mind sometimes, when I'm alone with my thoughts and lost in memories of gore and punishment.

My father had called it a gift for becoming a woman. I should have recognized how far gone I was then, but there was no one to keep me anchored. He encouraged my interests, even finding me experts to work with, allowing me to shadow his men on easier jobs before asking me to demonstrate what I'd learned. Like any child, I'd been proud of myself, pleased with how I could bring down a fully grown man with nothing more than a few drops of a home-made poison or eliminate a woman with the blade hidden in my heel, ending her life before anyone even realized there was an issue. Hiding my kills had been easy for my father, he always claimed credit and in doing so he kept me safe, gave me the armor I needed to protect myself from the others. We both failed to notice that I was losing myself to the bloodshed and violence like it was the air I needed to breathe. It was a larger part of me than either of us could have imagined. Rosalyn Gambino was more than just a Mafia princess in my father's mind, one day she was going to be Queen.

"Are you ready Rosie?" my father asks, his gentle voice revealing a side that is reserved solely for my mother and I. Vincent Gambino oozes power in his suit, dark hair slicked back, and a cheeky glint in his dark chocolate eyes. He was a wolf with a charming smile.

I smooth out imaginary creases on my soft cream gown and nod. I'd been preparing for this evening for years, and my parents had always been open about what they expected from me.

My mother kisses my forehead, and I'm enveloped in the soft scent of roses as she holds me. She's regal in her green velvet dress, dark red lipstick and her thick blonde hair perfectly coiffed. She's every inch an Italian beauty despite her coloring, her curves and beauty envied by the other wives and girlfriends. They whispered about her when they thought she wasn't listening, talking about her 'mixed-blood' because my grandmother had been a model from Wales, in the US for work when she met my Italian grandfather. There was no denying our heritage, not when we were both blonde with blue eyes in a world of deep rich browns, russet tones and chestnut hues. She's been another princess, like me, born with a mark already on her back and a knife at her throat. She wore her status like a crown, standing tall and proud beside my father like the perfect wife she was.

Tonight is a special occasion for The Family. Not only is it my eighteenth birthday party, but it's also the night my father aligns our family with the Asaro family. Their son, Julian, is two years older than me and currently studying law in college, following in his father's footsteps. The Asaro family owns most of the shipping businesses along with a few transport companies here in Newtown, and my father is desperate to align with them in any way possible. Even if it means bartering with his only child.

If the two families combined, we could rival the power of the current Don, Frank Belcastro, a vindictive son of a bitch who is currently the head of what we call 'The Family'. Frank was a greedy, hungry, beast of a man who had no concept of morality or loyalty. He took what he wanted, when he wanted. My father killed because they had disrespected or wronged him, he never took a life carelessly. Frank killed because he liked the color red, he wanted to bathe in the ruby liquid like some kind of deranged vampire, as if it gave him more power. Not that Felix Asaro was rumored to be much better. The wives often talked about Lina Asaro, and how she covered her bruises with scarves and sunglasses as if that would make them vanish. Her husband was often unfaithful as well as nasty, if the whispers were founded in truth. Out of sight, out of mind was an accepted mentality amongst some of the women and I refused to live like that. That's why I learned, it's why I waited.

I understand what has to happen for The Family to be rid of Frank, and I know what my role is even though I always thought I was worth more than just my name and my body. My wants are negated in this matter, I'm simply to smile and win over Julian Asaro. When that is done, then it will be my time to reign. I feel like it should be easy, but there's an unease in my stomach that won't settle. My father might be about to use me like a pretty pawn, and I might be going along with his wishes, but once I was married, my life would be on my terms.

So why does it feel like there's a knot, getting tighter and tighter with every step we take towards the reception room? I was ready for this. I am eighteen, a woman now. A strong, deadly woman. I had nothing to fear, not when I was Rosie Gambino. But I still couldn't shake that sliver of unease.

Holding out his arm for me to take, my father leans down and whispers, "Do you have your garter?"

He isn't referring to a piece of lingerie, he's talking about the discrete gold band he gifted me earlier in the day with a diamond-encrusted stiletto blade that's now pressed against the outside of my thigh. My mother had rolled her eyes as I'd gushed over the weapon, knowing that it was useless to protest, while my father had chuckled. It's both beautiful and deadly, much like me he had said as I opened the box. This Family isn't quite like others, but I don't know any other kind. Nodding, I pull him tighter against me in a half hug before we head downstairs ready to greet our guests for the evening.

The party is being hosted in our family mansion on the outskirts of Newton. It's a large Georgian style building, with acres of land surrounding us on all sides, the backyard leading out into the woods with a small stream. My mother designed the interior, and each room has her stamp on it, from the cherrywood floors to the intricate chandeliers. The house had been in her family for generations, and when she married my father at the tender age of eighteen, my grandparents had gifted it to them as a wedding present. It always made me feel like some sort of regency princess, rather than an angel of death as my father sometimes jokingly called me. It was a home filled with love and laughter, as long as you didn't look too closely, because that's when you noticed the blood-spattered carpets. Family life was ingrained into our daily life, like violence and bloodshed were normal.

Smiling, I nod towards several of the men who served alongside my father, their faces as recognizable to me as my own since I'd grown up with them coming and going from our house. A few of them even trained me, worked with me under my father's supervision, of course. They were like family, and not just because they were part of The Family. My father is quickly drawn into conversation to my left and vanishes into the crowd gathered here tonight, while my mother makes her way through the double doors to my right to where some of the wives have set up camp in our drawing room, their champagne glasses being dutifully refilled by the staff on site this evening.

I move through the rooms, swaying softly to the music the orchestra plays until I spot my grandmother near the kitchen. I make light conversation with her for a while and accept her gift of a beautiful new hair pin, before I make another circuit around the room, stopping as well-wishers congratulate me and admire my gown. My nonna Maria, my father's mother, is a grumpy old woman who prefers her own company, despite how hard my mother goes out of her way to try and include her in all our family events. I was surprised she'd decided to attend this evening, since she never seemed to particularly like me or my mother. The pin she gifted me was beautiful, an antique piece with a ruby flower adorning the end and two smaller stones dangling off a silver chain. Maybe there was something about becoming a woman that softened the old bat towards me.

"*Belissima*, Rosie!" Alessio, my father's oldest friend says as he spots me in the crowd and pulls me in for a hug. He spins me, making my dress twirl around my legs as I turn before I laugh and stop, facing him. His dark eyes burn into mine as he takes my hands in his, quickly inspecting my fingers before gently letting them fall back to my sides. "Playing with the silver nitrate again, *bambina*?"

I shrug, avoiding answering his question since my

father didn't want me to showcase my skills. But this was Alessio, the man who'd helped me learn about toxic plants and which chemical compounds could kill a man almost instantly. Family politics was still a little beyond me, since father said I was too trusting, so it was best to keep my distance where I could and simply steer clear of anything that could incriminate me.

"A little ammonia will take care of that," he offers as the corners of my mouth tug up into a grin. He lifts an eyebrow knowingly before grinning in return.

"Stop encouraging her, Alessio!" my mother chides, as she sashays past in a cloud of perfume and laughter. "Come, Rosalyn. Your father is busy with *zio* Renato in his office, but your *zio* Matteo has just arrived and he's brought you a gift."

My uncle Matteo was responsible for making sure that the 'produce' moved through Newtown smoothly, without being intercepted or delayed. Since he was the one who taught me to shoot a gun, I'd always assumed that the 'produce' meant firearms, but recently I'd overheard snippets of conversation from my father's office that told me drugs were Matteo's specialty. And also, his weakness. Even at eighteen, I knew you didn't sample your own product. It made him increasingly unpredictable and unstable according to what my parents discussed in hushed tones when they thought I was tucked away in bed. Tonight, is about me, and the Asaro family, so I store away the rumors and whispers for another day.

"Go!" Alessio shoos me away towards my mother. "The birthday girl must socialize. *Buon compleanno*, Rosie."

After another hour of making polite conversation and being kissed by various Captains, I decide I need a breather. I make my excuses to my parents and slip out into the garden, ignoring the soldiers and other Family members milling around. The knot in my stomach has done nothing but grow, getting tighter and bigger through-out the evening and it feels like something is wrong, but I can't put my finger on it. Was it the fact my father wanted me to marry a man I didn't know? No, I'd known my whole life that this was the path I might have to take. I'd been prepared for it. This feeling was like an unrest in my core and I wasn't used to this. I was trained not to hesitate, not to think twice. Felix Asaro had barely looked in my direction all evening and his wife, sporting another fancy scarf, had only given me weak, soft smiles. Their son was nowhere to be seen. I wasn't surprised. Arranged marriage, while the norm amongst The Family, wasn't a pill easily swallowed and the ballroom has been busy, almost bursting at the seams as the entire Family came out to watch and drink our champagne. I don't really recall Julian Asaro from my childhood, which is strange as we would have grown up around one another. Then again, my father did try his best to keep me separate from the other Family children. He'd called them all 'pawns in a game they couldn't begin to comprehend', ignoring the fact that I too was just another piece on the chessboard.

Sighing, I take a seat upon a bench near the roses my mother carefully nurtures. The enclosed rose garden was surrounded by large trees, for privacy and also to block out the noise of the suburbs, just as my mother preferred it. We always joke that she has the most beautiful garden, because my father fertilized it with the bodies of the men who flirt with her. It isn't true, he has another site he likes to use to dispose of bodies, but his joke always makes my mother smile.

"Aren't you cold?" a husky voice calls through the bushes. A shiver runs through me as the cool air moves over my skin.

Standing, I tense, ready to attack as I wait for the speaker to emerge from the bushes. The dark shadows swirling across the greenery trick my brain into thinking that there's more than one person lurking in the darkness as I struggle to locate the intruder.

A young man steps forward, his dirty blonde hair is gently ruffled and sharp green eyes watch me cautiously. He looks familiar, his face reminding me of someone but I can't place him. There are a few young men here this evening, all desperate to impress their Captains, my father and of course, Frank. All of them watched me in the ballroom like I was their meal ticket, their way into earning favors, but unfortunately for them I was already promised to another.

I answer brusquely, "No, I'm fine."

"Do you mind if I join you?" he asks, motioning for us both to sit and for some reason I do. I don't know why. He doesn't make alarm bells ring in my head as he gives me a ghost of a smile. Instead, he makes me feel...oddly safe out here in the dark. In all likelihood, I'm probably the most dangerous thing lurking out here tonight, not that you can tell with all my pretty packaging.

Dragging my nails over the cream fabric of my gown, I squint, trying to make out the sharp angles of his face in the shadows. "Who are you?"

He must be from one of the other families, or maybe part of the serving staff for tonight. A nagging in my head makes me growl softly in frustration. I feel like I should know him, but nothing comes to mind. There's no one else in attendance tonight with his coloring either, that golden hair glinting in the low lighting like a halo around his head. My gaze catches on a pair of expensive silver cufflinks shining in the dark, not staff then.

Moving closer, some of the darkness falls away and in the moonlight I'm able to see more of his beautiful face. And he is beautiful, especially given the crowd gathered tonight. There's something softer about him, kinder than the hard faces of the men in The Family.

"You can call me Jay, and you are?" His words make me shiver again, I really should have brought a shawl or something out with me. It was silly to react to someone like this, cliched, like something out of those damn romance novels my mother read.

No surname. Interesting. In an organization where everyone knows everyone it wasn't uncommon not to bother with surnames, but at a first meeting it meant he was hiding something. He didn't want me to know who he was and to which family he belonged, he was keeping his allegiances a secret. Again, not unusual in the world we lived in. It meant he saw me as a potential threat.

Copying his nonchalant tone, I stretched out my legs. "Rosie."

His eyes followed the movement, his gaze meandering up the length of my body before settling on my face. Grinning as he removes his tie, he gives a soft sigh. "I hate parties like this, they're always boring."

Raising an eyebrow at him, I cross my arms and lean back. He thought Mafia business was boring? Didn't he realize what a hotbed of gossip, sex and scandal events like this were? These parties and events were literally the only thing that broke up the monotony of my days, which were filled with training —both weapons and martial arts, school, and my family. I had no friends, they were just a distraction, so I lived for these events.

"Then why did you come?" I ask with a tilt of my head, only mildly insulted that he didn't seem to recognize me as Rosalyn Gambino at my own birthday party.

"Family business," he smirks, as he crosses his legs and leans back, looking up at the night sky. The best part of living on the outskirts of the city is the night sky. Above us the sky is like a glittering blanket, shimmering and blinking like thousands of diamonds scattered in the blackness.

I can't help myself as I snort, "Punny."

My mother often joked that my sense of humor was awful, like my father's but she always said it with a soft smile. I was an eighteen-year-old girl living in a dark, depraved world, so what did I have if not my humor and my looks? Those were the things that would keep me sane, while my hunger for violence and my talent for murder would keep me alive. I was lethal and the boy next to me was oblivious to it all.

"I do try," he replies, the corner of his mouth twitching. He has a dimple on the left side of his mouth, and I find myself staring at it when he whispers, "Do you ever want something different?"

The loneliness playing on his shadowed features make my chest constrict as I think about his question. The Family was my life. My mother, family, even my old goat Nonna were all I'd ever known and I was happy living here with them. I liked making them proud. I excelled at my training and in school, but was I willing to give that up to marry Julian Asaro and become a trophy wife? My father thought he was arming me, protecting me, giving me options, but if I thought about it for too long, if I looked too deeply, I realized I was still trapped in the same patriarchal, chauvinistic world run by men with money and guns.

My tongue feels heavy as I say, "This is all I've ever known."

He leans in toward me so that our shoulders are touching as we both watch the twinkling stars. The warmth from his body is like a slow burn, seeping into my bones from where our bodies connect. "And how does it feel? Honestly?"

"Empty." I frown as the word slips from my lips. I don't know why I said that. I don't know what possessed me. I was happy with my life, I was spoiled, I never wanted for anything and one day I'd be running the organization, even if it would be on the arm of my husband. I was happy. Happy. I say that word a million times in my head, but what exactly did happiness feel like? I *was* happy. Wasn't I? Flustered and feeling like I've said something wrong, I jump to my feet. My throat feels tight, and the heady scent of my mother's roses are beginning to overwhelm me. I need to go back inside where my head is on my shoulders straight and I'm not distracted by a stranger with emerald eyes.

"Wait." He grabs my hand as he stands. "Stay just a little longer."

I say nothing as he takes my other hand and we stand toe to toe in the moonlight.

"Rosie," he whispers before leaning in, "Dance with me?"

Through the various open windows and the open patio doors, I can faintly hear the orchestra still playing, but it isn't loud enough for me to be able to follow along with the song. I hesitate, just watching him.

"Don't overthink it, just dance with me." He doesn't give me the chance to refuse as his hand comes around my waist and pulls me flush against his chest. He smells like saltwater, crisp and cool with a hint of something else, something darker, spicier. Using his other hand, he guides my hand to his shoulder and it's like my body automatically responds, clasping my hands together behind his neck.

The heat of his hands splayed across my back, through the thin silk of my dress makes me exhale shakily. I'd never been this intimate with someone, never wanted to be. I built walls to keep them away and to keep myself safe. I knew my future was pre-planned so it was never worth the heartbreak. My life belonged to The Family.

"Did you know that skeletons hate parties?" he says, his voice low as we sway together in the gardens. Everything felt like some sort of out of body experience in that moment, like a wild dream where I was going to wake any second.

I hold onto him a little tighter, not wanting whatever this was to end yet. "Huh? Skeletons?"

He nods, bringing his face inches away from mine. "They have no body to dance with."

We stare at each other for a moment, before we

both laugh. When the sound slowly fades, I realize he's resting his forehead against mine. Why does this feel right? As if I'm meant to be in his arms? I've never been kissed before; I'd never been interested and at school I'd always felt like I was different from everyone else there. But I want this. I want him. As his lips touch mine, it's like all my coherent thoughts scatter to the furthest reaches of my mind. There exists only him in this moment. His warm hands cup my cold cheeks as he deepens the embrace, eager to taste me and I feel myself relax into him, sinking into his hard, warm body...and that's when I hear gunshots.

I try to pull away but his fingers dig into my skin, holding me in place. He keeps my face pressed against his as he murmurs against my lips, "Don't go...please."

Screams fill the air as I try to pull away. More gunshots fire. People pour out of the house like rats fleeing a sinking ship, scrambling and wailing. His soft pleas, the heat from his body, the sickly smell of roses and blood. It's like someone has poured a bucket of ice on me as I feel chilled to the bone. Numb. He was nothing more than a charming distraction. A traitor.

Reaching down, I grab my stiletto dagger from the garter, and press it into his neck. The sharp point breaks the skin so that a ruby red droplet trickles down the blade, and for a moment I watch, mesmerized. Even bleeding he's beautiful.

"Let go," I hiss finally, putting more pressure on the blade as his hands slip from my face. I turn, and he grabs my wrist.

"Rosie...don't go. Don't do this to yourself..." He stands dejected, guilt etched on his face so clearly I could kick myself for not noticing it earlier.

This time I don't hesitate as I stab the hand clutching at me. I ignore the grunt he makes as he tries to cling onto me, even though my knife is sliding into the back of his hand like he was made of play dough.

"You've done this," I growl, as I pull the blade out and wipe it on my skirt. He clutches his injured hand to his chest, trying to stem the bleeding. "Whatever happens after this is on you, Jay. I hope you can live with that."

Ten Years Later . . .

Chapter One
Julian

"Sir, it appears that the 'Queen of Hearts' is at it again. Three dead downtown." Daniel, my assistant, clears his throat softly before dropping some files onto my desk. He runs a hand through his dark chestnut hair avoiding my gaze and I know it's because he's been reluctant to inform me of this latest development, but I had been expecting it.

Leaning back in my plush leather chair, I glance over at the calendar resting on my oak desk. May the eighth. Right on time.

Daniel places a coffee before me, and finally gives me a pitying look. He knows the score by now since he'd been with me for years, but it still didn't make him less nervous when he had to tell me about the Queen's antics. He was a little too soft to work for me, but I'd hired him all the same. A slight, anxious man with big brown eyes hidden behind a pair of round glasses and messy hair, he was unoffensive and seemed to make a lot of my clients feel relaxed, especially since I was usually surrounded by mean-looking mother fuckers.

Glancing out the window, I take in Newtown in all its early morning glory. This city was my home, with its hustle and bustle, from the dark and seedy side run by The Family, to the picture-perfect suburbs filled with happy families and wealthy businessmen. All of it fell under my domain as the current Don or 'Father' of the Family. Eli and I had called it 'Wonderland' jokingly once after a night with too much tequila and it stuck. Newtown was a place filled with amazements and cruelty, brutality and beauty and from that, the WunderLnd Corporation was born. Ten years of honing my network, building relationships, investing in businesses, guiding The Family to where it was now and yet every year, on May the 8th, one woman undermined all of that.

Rubbing my forehead with a groan, I ignore my Left Hand, Elijah Creed chuckling on my sofa. He's tied his long hair back today, and dressed for the office, but the sharp cut of his suit does nothing to hide the menacing aura that clings to him like a second skin. Tattoos snake up his neck, across the exposed flesh on his chest and on his hands. The scar that splits his eyebrow neatly in two adds to the glare he gives me, the one that says 'Told you so!'

As my best friend, Eli thinks this is all just a funny game. As my Left Hand, he thinks I should have killed her a long time ago and put an end to these petty gifts of hers. I'm well aware that if I don't get her under control soon, I'll have a bigger issue than some dead retired gangsters.

People were supporting her and slowly, each year she was gaining more influence. They protected her, hid her, funded her and kept her off my radar. The people who were supposed to be MY people protected her. It undermined me, and sowed seeds of dissent amongst the ranks. I wasn't a fool, I knew that before long if she kept this up, she'd be running The Family. I'd had to protect and pledge allegiance to several of the men who'd carried out the massacre with my father and Frank that night ten years ago. I said I would protect them, swore to them that I would and yet each year some of them died.

"Hearts?" I ask, even though I already know the answer. There's a reason the press and the rest of the

Family have dubbed her the 'Queen of Hearts', and it's not because she's a generous, giving woman. She's a devil who likes to get her hands dirty.

Another awkward cough as Daniel's face pales. "Removed."

I could expect another article in the news tomorrow talking about the crazy Queen of Hearts whose identity has yet to be discovered after all these years. There were conspiracy theories of course, there always were. But since nothing could ever be linked back to me, and I made sure Creed disposed of the evidence making me just another concerned citizen of Newtown. Those bodies simply became empty shells, with missing hearts. I wonder if she really did remove them herself, or if she made one of her minions do it. No one outside of this room and the crazy bitch herself, knew that they were in an ornate box on my assistant's desk.

"You know the drill," I sigh, waving my hand at Daniel, knowing that he's now going to scrub his desk within an inch of its life, and I'm going to deposit a fat bonus in his account to make up for it. "I'm going to wring her neck when I get my hands on her."

I feel Eli slap my shoulder affectionately. "Why don't you just let me kill her Jules?"

He leans back to sit on the edge of my desk, as we

both look out the window in brooding silence for a few moments. He's my closest friend, the Left Hand of The Family. It's his job to clean up these messes and protect our organization but she is different. I can't bring myself to dispose of her so easily.

"Because if you kill Rosalyn Gambino, then I'm no better than my father." I bury my head in my hands. I'm not just the head of this organization, I'm also a lawyer and from one of the most influential families in this city. I'm in the public eye regularly, so my extra-duties as the head of The Family need to be kept quiet. There are only three people I trust completely, one of them is dead, one is currently perched on my desk and the other is outside cleaning up my messy history. I don't even give Janice, my receptionist for the last five years the same level of trust as I do them.

"Who's dead?" I ask even though the list of possible candidates has grown considerably smaller over time. Initially it had seemed like the kills were random, just another way to get back at my father and Frank Belcastro for what they took from her that night. And they took everything. I don't even know how she managed to survive, how she escaped and yet she did. It wasn't until we dug a little deeper, we realized they'd all been present that night. The dead men had all helped us destroy the Gambino branch of the Family in some way, and she knew it.

"Lewis Salvatore, Frankie Rossi and Roy Palma," Eli says as he looks at the tablet Daniel left behind.

Fuck. Salvatore and Rossi had both been my father's bodyguards ten years ago and as for Palma— he'd been the head of Gambino security. "How do we know, Creed?"

"Their bodies were identified an hour ago." He checks his phone, his contact in the police department no doubt confirming the details Daniel had given us.

"Were they reported missing?" How had three of my men been killed without a peep? Without even a ripple in Newtown of them being missing?

Part of Creed's role was to keep track of various members, and although he didn't appear fastidious with his duties, he was. He shrugs, before launching into an explanation. "The Rossi family have gone into hiding; Frankie's sons are believed to be somewhere in China. Salvatore was a drunk who often went missing for days at a time and Palma lived off the grid with his male lover."

The Rossi's were entitled assholes, but smart. If they were on the run, then they knew what was coming. They hadn't come to me for my protection like the others, and now it was out of my hands.

Salvatore's widow would collect a nice little payout from his death which should clear the gambling debts he'd accrued through his drinking habits. That was one less worry on my plate with his death at least. Even though I had no issues with anyone's sexuality, older fractions of The Family still held on to traditionalist views which meant Roy had been pushed out slowly until he was living, isolated from the people he'd served his whole life. Pushing the intercom, I ask Daniel to return to my office when he's done wiping down his work space. I'll need him to follow up with the widow and the lover just to ensure they were provided for. These were still my people. Every year her targets were getting closer to the center, closer to me. I'm pretty sure her plan was to save me for last.

"And you're sure it's her, Sir?" Daniel asks as he enters my office with more paperwork for my already crammed schedule for today, pushing his glasses back up his nose as he shuffles toward my desk.

My intercom system buzzes, Janice's voice crackles through the speakers. "There's a delivery down here at reception for you, Sir."

I ignore Daniel's words. Of course, it's her. Who else would mail me the hearts of three of my soldiers on the anniversary of her parents' death?

"Deal with it, Eli." I cover my face and turn away

from the window. Fuck. Had Rosie lost her damn mind? When was she going to give up with these stupid little games? Her family was gone. Belcastro and my father were gone. Was it really worth dedicating her whole life to this?

Eli nods. "As always Julian, but I still don't get why you don't just kill her. Death is a much more satisfactory action here."

"Because . . ." *I don't want to.* "Because I'm going to handle this."

Creed narrows his eyes at me for a second and shrugs before leaving the office. He's been by my side my entire life; he knows that I'm avoiding what must be done because I don't want to repeat my father's sins. I wanted to be different from him, I wanted to rein in the bloodthirsty nature of our Family. I'm not naive, I know that being the head of the mafia means having to make decisions that get my hands dirty, but I also know that violence is slowly losing its power to money and I plan to use that. I want to move us forward.

The world Eli and I grew up in was vastly different to the one we oversee now. We are not the monsters who raised us. I would never cause pain for fun, unlike my father. Felix Asaro was a violent man, who only knew how to communicate with his fists. Like all children in The Family, death and destruction was the norm. I killed my first man when I was only twelve, and when I'd thrown up afterwards, my father had laughed before making me clean it up. My teenage years were spent reluctantly witnessing and partaking in gruesome crimes, and watching the fallout as we returned home and my father beat me for my 'pussy-ways'. Except I wasn't a pussy, I was a kid. A kid who others congratulated and admired. Frank Belcastro, our Don even praised me for being the kind of man they needed in The Family, but all my father saw was flaws.

When I finally managed to claw my way to the top and move us away from all the needless bloodshed, Rosie reminded me exactly of all those cracks in my armor. She dug her nails into all of my flaws and wormed her fingers in deeper until I bled. Miss Gambino was gaining a reputation since she's the embodiment of the 'old ways', where force and violence equate to strength according to my Captains, and that's why she was growing a following. People want bloodthirsty, they want power and if she looks anything like she did ten years ago, I'm willing to bet that being beautiful doesn't hurt her campaign.

That night haunts me, I still dream about it some-times. Those nights are the worst because when I wake, sweaty, heart beating so hard it hurts, I swear I can still smell her mother's roses. The look of utter betrayal on her face is burned into my mind, those big blue eyes hurt as she connects the dots and brands me a traitor. I rub my thumb over the scar on my hand absent-mindedly. They say that the road to hell is paved with good intentions, and they're right. I tried to save her from the mess, to distract her, to keep her safe from my father and outside with me away from the gunfire. But it backfired.

It was a massacre that night, one that's gone down in the history of this city as Newtown's most violent homicide. Rosie should have been amongst the dead. She was supposed to be. Her death was intended to mark the end of the Gambino line but somehow, she emerged, covered in blood and has been a thorn in my side since then.

My father did everything he could to extinguish her in the following years, but the Gambino family still had powerful friends in rich circles. Her survival seemed to rally some of the others, and they saw her as an avenging angel. Furious, Felix did the only thing he could, he took away her money. Her home. He made the Gambino's traitors and then he made her persona non grata. He thought this would make her crawl back and beg for forgiveness. He was wrong. It was a trick that's coming back to bite me in the ass now that I can't track her down and her name is nothing more than a whisper amongst my peers and my men. She's a ghost Queen, a legend, tearing out hearts and hiding in the shadows as she rallies an army against me.

Creed comes back into the room, a card in his hand. He hands it to me with a pointed look, he wants to torture her. To break her into a million little pieces and scatter them off the nearest bridge for the problems she's caused. A part of me wants that too, and the other part feels guilt. I turn the card over in my hands, knowing we won't find any fingerprints or evidence on it. She's too good for that. It's white, and perfectly clean apart from one corner where blood has started to seep through the paper. It must have been in contact with the contents of the box at some point. I run my fingers over her neat calligraphy.

Jay,
I hope my gift finds you safely.
Enjoy.
Love, R x

I didn't want to kill her, but if she didn't stop with these attacks on The Family, then she'd leave me with no other choice. My Captains were already calling for her head on a platter as one of my Captains, Lawrence liked to remind me. Daily. Repeatedly. Like I was some naive little child, and not the head of a powerful organization, a billionaire, a businessman, a lawyer and an advocate for Newtown. To leave her unpunished showed weakness, and as the head of The Family, I couldn't show any hesitation.

Even if Rosie Gambino was once almost my wife.

Even if I ruined her life.

Chapter Two

Rosie

"Did he get the gift?" I ask down the phone as I stretch out on my bed for the evening. The naked man next to me snoring away, oblivious to my conversation and the fact I drugged him. Poison was my forte, I guess you could say it was something I'd shown talent for from a young age. My tio Alessio had made sure I could protect myself, even after my parents died. It was also less messy than a gun or a knife, and I typically hated getting my hands dirty.

Julian Asaro, however, was the exception to that rule. For him I wanted to get more than just my hands dirty. I wanted to bathe in his blood. I wanted it to congeal on my skin, until it itched and flaked away, leaving me to emerge like an avenging butterfly. I wanted it under my nails, making everything feel dirty and grimy. I was owed a messy painful death.

The man beside me snorts in his sleep. Tonight, I wasn't in the mood to be groped and molested by a man who claimed to have a solid nine inches but actually only had four. Still, he was useful for a place to sleep instead of crashing back at Lola's tiny cramped apartment again, not that I wasn't grateful to my best friend. She was the only person I trusted in the world, but she was having troubles of her own in the form of a handsome bald stalker with serious 'Daddy' vibes.

Rolling my eyes, I push the guy whose name I can't remember further to the edge of the bed with my foot. I'd picked him up at The Top Hat, the gentlemen's club downtown where Lola worked. It was a gaudy, over the top club with red lighting and pink neon signs run by The Family. Risky, but sometimes the best hiding places are the most obvious ones. It was the main reason Julian hadn't been able to catch-up with me so far and it made our little cat and mouse game that much more thrilling.

Really, The Top Hat was a brothel, but over the

years Julian had brought in more regulations, better safety measures for the girls who worked there and it had improved the joint a little. The 'Flowers' were still whores, but at least now they had the option to refuse their clients. Besides, May the eighth is exclusively for Jay Asaro. He owns this date every year and it's almost like it's become special in its own twisted way and not just because it's the anniversary of my parents' death.

The soft voice on the other end of the line hesitates, "Yes."

I grin. I bet he was pissed when he read the card even though I'd used my best handwriting. "Good."

"I really think he's going to kill you soon." The voice trembles and it gives me goosebumps as I imagine his hands around my throat, choking the life out of me. As if Julian could kill me. Flicking through the magazine on the nightstand, I pause when I come across an article about the great Julian himself, arriving at a swanky charity dinner with some glamour model. She's beautiful, with dark hair and big hazel eyes but there's no chemistry between them. He's a perfect gentleman, his hand never dipping below her waist and almost hovering inches away from her skin as if he's afraid touching her might burn. There's never been anyone serious, not since our supposed engagement and I don't have to wonder why that is. He's afraid. He's afraid that if he falls in love, I'll take that away from him too just like I'm slowly stealing away The Family and his precious WunderLnd Corporation. If I have to be alone in this world, then so does he. It's only fair.

"I'd like to see him try." Tracing my finger over his strong jawline and sharp nose, I smile. "In fact, we may be overdue a catch-up."

Silence. Followed with a soft begging, "Please don't do anything stupid..."

I groan, "Don't whine. I have no patience for that."

More silence. I wait, patiently, which is not admittedly one of my finer qualities.

Finally the voice offers, "He's got another charity ball next week. At Newtown Plaza Hotel."

I look at the image of Julian in a tux once again, and a heat unfurls in my stomach at the thought of seeing him in person for the first time in years. "And you can get me tickets?"

"Of course. But are you sure? There'll be lots of security, and Creed will be there with him." Elijah Creed. Julian's 'Left Hand', his most loyal supporter and his best friend. He was on my list, near the very top but I was saving him for last. Well, Jay was last, so Creed would have to be the penultimate kill.

"Good job," I praise, even though it frustrates me that he's second guessing me. I can handle the security issues. Everyone has a price, it's just a matter of finding it. "Check your phone, I'll send you something as a reward."

Hanging up without waiting for his response, I take a picture as a little sweetener to offer up. I make sure that only part of my face and hair is visible, not enough to identify me, but enough to verify that it's me while the rest of the shot focuses over my shoulder. I look over the image, the dim lighting flattering the curves of my body, my ass and toned legs, looking almost sinful as I lay on my stomach amongst the black bedding, my bed partner just out of shot. I send it and turn the phone off without another thought of the person on the other end.

Some relationships were forged through shared hardships, through blood, others through an alignment of goals and ones like this...they were made under delusions of love. He worshipped me, and if my father had taught me anything, it was to use every tool in your arsenal. I flick on the TV and catch up on my favorite baking shows before drifting off for a few hours of uninterrupted sleep, a grin plastered on my face at the thought of Julian Asaro bleeding in his tux.

T he shots are so loud they reverberate around my house. It's like a sensory overload as my brain struggles to process what's happening. There are people everywhere, pushing and shoving desperate to escape. They move like an angry swarm, swelling and pulsing around me.

Screams.

Shouts.

More screams.

I tear through the kitchen calling for my parents. Someone tries to grab me, but I thrust my blade into their side. I don't even check to see who I've hurt. No one can get in my way; I need my parents. I shout so much that my throat burns. It feels raw, like I've swallowed glass as I call for my mother. How could I have let myself get distracted by a pretty face? I should have known better. I was taught better. Warm blood trickles down my arm as I duck into our dining room where most of the guests had been gathered. I'm not sure if it's my blood or someone else's. It doesn't matter. My parents should be here. But I can't see them. Panic rises in my chest and I suck in big gulps of air. Calm, Rosie. Calm. It doesn't work. There are dead bodies on our floor, bleeding all over my mother's favorite rug. Crimson soaking into the threads, tainting everything. Ruining everything. Don't be dead, I plead silently as I check their clothing and faces. Not my parents. They were someone's parents, but they weren't mine. Don't be dead. My father was going to be furious when he saw the mess. Please, don't be dead.

I don't know who opened fire. I don't even know who is firing. I can't tell who is on what side but this family has been torn apart. I see my uncles, Captains and men I smiled at only hours ago, killing one another. Blasting holes in the walls of my home. Destroying the house my mother decorated so lovingly. My grandmother's body sits slumped, still in her chair in the corner, half her skull missing and I swallow painfully. Please. Please. Don't let my parents be dead, I beg the god I no longer believe in. The Family was fractured and I don't understand why. Where is my father?

I hear voices above my head and with my blade still clutched in my hand I take the stairs two at a time. A hulking figure with a scarred face steps out of one of the rooms. I recognize him as one of Frank's men, and I vaguely remember my father praising him for being one of the best fighters at The Gryphon, the underground fighting ring. As he stands before me, blocking my way, I can see why. He's huge, all muscle and unrestrained anger. It radiates off him in waves, turning my stomach, and setting off alarm bells in my head. This is a man who enjoys pain, who lives for the destruction The Family offers.

He scoffs when he sees me. Face twisted into a nasty snarl that I'll never forget.

"Come here pretty princess," he hisses and with a growl he lunges at me. If I let him catch me, I don't even want to imagine what will happen. But it won't come to that because like the others, he underestimates me. Quickly, I stomp on his foot with my heel and when he bows into the unexpected pain, I ram my thin blade into his eye socket, forcing my weight behind it just like my father showed me. There's a sickening squelching noise as I destroy his eye. It's more than enough of a distraction as he howls and yanking the knife back out, I push him down the stairs hard with my foot. When I peer over the rail, his body lies at the bottom, bent and broken, head cracked open like a coconut with one glassy eye staring up at me, the other a pulpy socket.

Heading towards my father's office I stop in my tracks. The door is partially open and I can see them on their knees. My parents. Tears streamed down my mother's face as my father held her hand. Her blonde hair is a mess, the artful chignon she wore earlier in the evening gone. A dark purple blossom forms around her eye, and her lip is split, ruby red and swollen with blood. His expression is stoically blank. A gash along his cheek and cut to his eyebrow are *the only obvious wounds, but the way he holds himself carefully on one side makes me think he's nursing a few broken ribs. But they're alive.*

Men tear apart the room, throwing papers and books everywhere as they look for something. Sheafs of paper rain down like snow as the thud of books landing on the hardwood floors make me flinch.

More screams and guttural howls from downstairs distract me for a moment and when I look back my father's gaze locks with mine. He's seen me. He looks away quickly, at whoever is holding a gun on them. They're standing out of view but I can see the gun, and large masculine hands. My gut instinct said it was Felix, but unless I pushed the door open fully, I had no way of telling. Creeping closer, I try to get a better look but my father's head nods slightly, a sign telling me to leave. I can't go. Not now. I have to do something. I can see hands now, a fancy silver cufflink in the shape of a snake catches in the light and the edge of a tattoo. I need more. I need help. I count three different voices in the room besides the one with a gun on my parents. If I had any hope of getting them out of there, I needed to draw them out to divide and conquer. I couldn't just charge in there with my tiny little blade, not against their guns, even if I did have the element of surprise on my side.

I need to create a distraction that will get some of them

out of the room. *I can do this.* I shake my head at my father, I am not leaving. I won't. I can see his shoulders deflate as he realizes that I'm going to be my usual stubborn self. He nods his head again, knowing that it's inevitable now that I'm here. My mother sobs harder, but as her head turns, I know she's spotted me too.

Her eyes widen, and I know seconds before she opens her mouth what she's going to do. Throwing herself at the gun, she screams, "Run, Rosie! Run!"

Bang.

Bang.

Thud.

I watch her body fall to the ground and it's like my world moves in slow motion. Her eyes close as her head hits the rug and I know without a doubt that she'll never open them again. She's gone.

"Rosie!" my father screams and there's something about the desperation in his voice that snaps me out of my stupor. *I need to get away. If I survive, I can make them pay for this. I can come back for him... I can try... I can fight... I can...*

Bang.

I've never moved so fast in my life. I run. I run until I don't know where I am. Until my feet bleed. Until I can't move another step.

I never even saw his body land on the floor beside my mother's.

I never even said goodbye.

Please.

Don't be dead, I sob.

Even though I know he is.

Chapter Three
Julian

"Remind me why I have to come to this stupid gala?" Eli grumbles as he tugs at his bow tie with a grunt. Once he's loosened that, he goes back to adjusting his black and silver masquerade mask. He hated wearing formal attire, and only wore a suit in the office because I'd insisted. Usually he wore boots, jeans and a worn T-shirt that wasn't even legible anymore but that wasn't going to cut it here at the Newtown Plaza hotel, one of the most exclusive venues in the city.

The ostentatious marble floors and huge black pillars made this the perfect place for a charity dinner. The theme had clearly been Venetian inspired, as decadent centerpieces with feathers and gold adorned every table. Opulent gift bags were placed at each seat, and a large orchestra played, filling the hall with beautiful music. The masquerade gala dinner was nothing more than an excuse for the rich and famous to peacock and preen, flaunting their wealth under the guise of doing good for the city. I shouldn't be so bitter, since my firm and my family were benefactors, but sometimes I didn't understand why donations couldn't be made without all the pomp and showboating. I mean, I wasn't any less generous out of a white mask with gold edge embellishments, so what was the point of it all?

Chuckling, I tilt my glass towards him. "Because not only are you my friend, but I also pay your salary. And as my bodyguard, you should be here. Protecting my body."

Snorting, Eli narrows his eyes at me through the mask's holes. "Did you get hit on the head when I wasn't looking?"

"No," I sigh. "I'm just not in the mood for all of this tonight. And my date is like an octopus."

I'd brought along an actress I'd met a few weeks ago, at the opening of a new bar called The Blue Caterpillar. I wasn't looking for a date when I met her, I'd been there scouting out the bar and getting to know the owners, the Volkov twins. Their father, Lev, was a weapons supplier for us, importing goods from Russia as part of his role in the Bratva. Lev however had been quiet recently, and we hadn't met in person for almost two years now and so I hoped I might run into him at the quaint new cocktail bar. No such luck, but Alexi Volkov did manage to introduce me to tonight's date, Maddison Miles. What I hadn't realized was that she was determined to make herself the next Mrs. Asaro, viewing my bachelor status as a challenge. She was hell-bent on getting her claws into me, and in the car on the way over I barely managed to keep my dick in my pants, not for lack of trying.

"Yeah, I noticed she was a little handsy." Eli's shoulders shake as he laughs, glancing over to our table where she's obviously gushing about me with another actress, whose face I recognize, but the name escapes me.

"A little?" I scoff as I order another scotch at the bar, where we're perched. I quickly knock it back and tap my hands on the counter for another. "If I didn't know she was from Fort Windermere I would have sworn she was some Hindu goddess, desperate to make me worship at her altar."

Every time I tried to move away it was like she grew another pair of hands. Hands that just kept stroking, and grabbing and pulling at me like she was trying to climb into my tux with me. Her lips against my skin as she whispered filthy things in my ear, despite Elijah being sat right next to us.

Eli gives her another look over, this one more appreciative as a flash of interest in his black eyes. "Hey man, don't knock it. Magic hands are always a bonus in my book."

"Yeah, well maybe you should dance with her then." I really didn't want to. I mean, I would, because I was a gentleman and it was all part of the persona of Julian Asaro, lawyer, philanthropist, and spokesperson for the city. Plus, it would look good in the gossip columns tomorrow, even if that reporter Oliver Staddon didn't know his ass from his elbow when he wrote about me. I guess I should be a little more grateful, since his articles seemed to imply I was a soft hearted man holding out for the 'one', rather than the truth which was I only had casual sex complete with signed NDA's because I had a mafia organization to run and an insane jilted teen bride stalking me.

"She isn't my date, and as you already pointed out-—I'm here to work." Handing me a glass of soda water, he gives me a look. One that says *'You're here to work too, lay off the whiskey.'*

"Fuck you," I growl under my breath as I accept the glass, even though the shit tastes like TV static and sadness.

Taking a deep breath, I turn towards a group of politicians a few feet away from us when one of them calls my name. "Gentlemen, a pleasure to see you all here this evening. And for such a great cause!"

And so, the schmoozing continues. I spend the next two hours shaking hands and talking to what feels like every single person in this room between food courses and drinks. My cheeks have been kissed, my back slapped, my hands have been shaken so much they now just move up and down on their own. My cheeks hurt from smiling and laughing at awful jokes, but this is who I am and what I do. And I do it excellently.

It isn't until the dancing begins that I realize I can't find Maddison and Eli has done his usual thing of vanishing into the shadows, trying to avoid socializing. Bastard. I suppose that lets me off the hook from the dancefloor for a while as I meander through the crowd back to the bar, letting out a small sigh as I manage to polish off another scotch without Eli breathing down my neck.

As I sit nursing a second sneaky glass, a petite brunette approaches me with a small smile. She's wearing a black strapless gown that hugs her ample figure, her cleavage inviting and decorated with gold chains that drape from a thick solid gold choker, across her collarbone and down over her bare shoulders. Her mask is the opposite to mine, but equally elegant in black with gold filigree embellishments. We look like a couple, like the embodiment of yin and yang, as she takes a seat at the bar beside me.

"Excuse me." Her voice is gentle and soothing, something about it echoes in my mind. "I hope you don't mind but your date had to step out and take a phone call, something about a new casting?"

I blink, privately relieved. "Oh, thank you for letting me know."

Looking up at me with big brown eyes, she bites down on her bottom lip nervously. The pink flesh is darker and swollen when she finally releases it. "Would you like to dance? I mean, just while your date is...otherwise occupied? I'm not sure if she's territorial over you, so I thought I would ask now, while I have the opportunity."

She grins and something about that makes me relax. Her gorgeous body doesn't hurt either. Maybe she'd be willing to fill in a non-disclosure and come home with me tonight? That is, if I could get

Maddison to give up on her insane quest to get her feet under my table.

"Have you been waiting for her to leave before you approached?" I tease, enjoying the way she nudges me with a soft laugh.

Offering her my arm, I lead us to the dancefloor where I don't hesitate to bring her into my chest and begin swaying us to the hypnotic medley the orchestra is playing. She smells like roses and cherries, there's a hint of cinnamon clinging to soft skin as I hold her in my arms.

We dance in silence, one song morphing into the next but I'm unwilling to end it yet. As the next song begins, I spin her out and pull her back into me once again, like she belonged with me. She throws her head back and laughs, and it makes my chest tighten. There's something oddly familiar about the small woman in my arms, something that feels like I've done this before. "Do I know you?"

"Hmmm, I don't know. Do you?" She tilts her head, and it's like it's there. On the periphery. Just out of reach.

She reminds me of that night. The smell of roses. The cinnamon. The little laugh. I spin her around, watching her carefully before putting my hands back on her waist. "You remind me of someone...but she was blonde. With green eyes."

"All things that can be easily changed Jay." Her voice is smoother now, less innocent as she pulls me closer. "Besides, I noticed you have a preference for brunettes and I wasn't sure you'd dance with me otherwise."

We're now dancing so close to one another that we're practically inches away from making out in front of all of Newtown's elite.

"Rosie?" I hiss, tightening my grip on her. "What the hell are you doing here?"

"Awh, is that any way to greet your ex-fiancé?" Her warmth breath tingles, skirting over my skin as she looks up at me, and it's killing me that half of her face is hidden by a stupid mask. Ten years. It's been ten years since that young girl in the garden had vanished, and now I wanted to see the depraved monster left behind. The one I helped create.

"My homicidal, insane ex, you mean? Besides, I'm not sure you even qualify as my ex. We didn't exactly know each other all that well." My voice is dripping with sarcasm, I hate being caught on the backfoot, unaware and that's exactly what she'd done. Why was it that I could run an entire empire in the shadowy depths of this city, under the noses of almost everyone in this room, and yet I managed to miss the woman in front of me because I was busy staring at her cleavage and her lips?

"Want to change that? I have no qualms about getting to know you more...intimately." Her tongue darts out, the pink tip swiping over her bottom lip. I'm ashamed and aroused as my dick twitches in my trousers. "I mean, it will suck when I finally get to the top of my list. But we'll get to make some fond memories before then."

Ah yes, nothing kills a boner quicker than a reminder that she actually wants to kill me. And yet, I still haven't let go of her.

The song changes again and we keep dancing. I keep my voice low and I lean in, and whisper against the shell of her ear. "I could have you arrested, hand you over to security."

She swallows, and I can't work out if it's nerves or just because we're in such close proximity. "For what?"

I step back, twirl her and bring her back in with my eyebrow raised. "For being the Queen of Hearts."

"And how would you prove it, Jay without giving yourself up at the same time?" The corner of her mouth pulls upwards. "Besides, I think you like this little game we play.""Don't be delusional. You're killing people." I know I'm frowning now, but I can't help it. I don't care who's watching, I just need to know if she really is as irredeemable as Eli thinks she is.

Pouting, she tries to give me sad eyes. "You don't like my gifts, Jay?"

"It's murder."

"It's retribution for a massacre." It's like a switch has been flipped as she straightens, and leans in closer. Her words are flat and cold. Despite her small stature, she's still an imposing figure somehow. Her mouth is now pulled straight, smile completely gone, as if she wasn't just flirting and making jokes two minutes before.

"Rosie..." I try to pull her flush against me, to offer her comfort but she resists.

"It doesn't seem so unwarranted now, does it," she hisses before biting on my earlobe sharply, the pain shooting down my neck as I try not to cause a scene or draw attention to us.

It proves pointless a moment later when a fire alarm begins blaring through the ballroom and everyone starts rushing towards the door.

"Ah, time's up!" She grins brightly, taking a step back and melting into the hysterical crowd. It's like I was dealing with two different people, I think to myself as I try to follow her. I can't keep her in my line of sight, her black clothing and height meaning she's easily swallowed up in the panic.

"What? Wait, Rosie—" I call out, my voice dying out as the alarms blared overhead.

"Jules, we need to get out of here!" Eli grabs my arm and starts pulling me with the crowd towards the door. He looks stressed, as we're pressed up against so many people, all pushing and shoving despite there being no actual fire in the ballroom. Didn't they realize we needed to exit calmly?

"Where the fuck have you been?" I shout at him, shaking him off. Frustrated that she'd been here, in my arms, and now in the blink of an eye she was gone again.

"I was with Maddison; she fell down some stairs in the foyer. Reckons she was pushed, so I was waiting with her and hotel security for the ambulance when the fire alarm started going off." Elijah looks at me, confused as he leads me out a side door, avoiding the circus in the hotel reception. As we jog down an alley-way, he makes a call and minutes later the car pulls up.

He starts checking me over once we are seated, making sure I'm alright before he grabs my chin and turns my head abruptly. "Fuck, what happened? Your ear is bleeding!"

Curling my hand into a tight fist, I grunt. "Rosie Gambino."

"Fuck." Eli sinks into his seat, not sure what else there is to say. The Queen of Hearts had been right in my hands, smelling like a freshly baked god-damn pie and I'd let her get away.

Fuck indeed.

Chapter Four

Rosie

"**Y**ou did what?!" Lola screeches before she bursts into laughter. "You can't just go around pushing his dates down stairs!"

I swallow the rest of my wine in two large gulps, "She tripped, Lola. Tripped."

My best friend snorts. "Yeah. Over your foot."

We're in her tiny kitchen, two days after the charity gala and I'm finally filling her in on how my evening went. I would have called her, but I tended not to use my phone very often since I cycled through burner phones quicker than I could count to ten. Besides, it was nice having someone excited to see me when I turned up on their doorstep. There were others, who offered me a bed and place to stay but they did it out of obligation to my parents or the belief that I should be running The Family. Lola wanted me here in her cramped little apartment because she missed me, because she loved me and that...that hurt as much as it lit me up.

The wine is making me morose, so I shake my head and crack an egg into the bowl she just handed me. "Are you going to help me make these cookies or not?"

"Still can't believe you've resorted to terrorizing his dates, Ro." She shakes her head and pushes aside the magazine we were looking at earlier in which a very sad looking Maddison Miles talks about her 'traumatic' evening at the hottest charity event in Newtown. She praises Julian for taking 'great care' of her even though I know he left her with the paramedics and did nothing more than send her a basket of fruit afterwards. Lying little toad.

Lola grabs a marker from the drawer as I mix in chocolate chips, and begins sketching out something on a sheet of paper. "And nope, I'm going to watch you make cookies while I make a sign to stick in my window for the creeper across the street."

I narrowed my eyes at her window and out into the darkness of the building opposite, as if I could see the stalker across the road, which I can't. But he doesn't know that. "Why don't you call the police on him."

Shrugging, she gives me a small smile. "He's not bothering me yet, just...watching."

I keep mixing before I cover the bowl and chill the mix in the fridge as she tapes the giant dick she's drawn to the window. "Hmmm, so no murder vibes then?"

"Rosie..." Glaring at me over her shoulder, she huffs. "Are you even allowed to ask that? You're my best friend and you actually murder people."

I kept very little from Lola because I'd never needed to. When I ran ten years ago, at eighteen years old, I ended up wandering the streets. Alone. Afraid. Covered in blood. I wasn't even sure if I was in Newtown anymore, and it turned out, I wasn't. I'd somehow, in a complete haze of grief and rage, made my way to East Point, a city a few hours away. That's where a bruised and scrawny, twenty-one-year-old Lola found me and took me in. She never asked whose blood I was wearing. Never demanded anything from me. Never made me explain anything. She simply took me as I was, and that was that.

We were best friends, found family—sisters. We even looked alike, both blonde although her eyes were green where mine were blue. And she was tall and leggy, whereas I was shorter and curvier. We milked it when we needed to, whether we used it as a story to lure men in before we robbed them or whether we said it simply to give each other comfort. It didn't matter. She was the only family I had left.

"People who deserve it," I remind her as I pour us both another glass of the cheap red wine she bought from the store. One day we'd have enough money to waste on nice wine and fancy glasses to drink from. One day when I took back what was rightfully mine.

"Irrelevant," she retorts as she grabs her glass and sinks down into the second-hand loveseat she bought at a garage sale a few weeks ago. We spoke about my family, and Julian often, but Lola never mentioned hers. When I wanted to move back here after living in East Point for a few years, she never even blinked. There was no one she had to say goodbye to and no one she talked about. Her only stipulation was that we avoided Aberfalls, and that we never went there and that was just fine by me.

"Do you want cookies or not?"

Watching me wipe down the counters and clean the dishes she tilts her head, thinking about it. "Are you using the cannabutter?"

My baking was legendary in her building and one

of her neighbors, a small-time dealer named Brad, had given us some cannabutter last week. I wink. "Nope, saving that for the brownies on the weekend."

My weekend plans consisted of special brownies, dancing and maybe a hot body to crawl into bed with. For a moment I picture Jay, stripping off his shirt, slowly. One button at a time, all seductive and sexy. The man is built, I could feel it when we danced, his muscles moving under my hands. For a moment I wonder if there's a way to lure him out with us on Saturday, but I know that's just wishful thinking. The man's so upstanding in public I bet he's never even experienced the nightlife in Newtown, not like he should. He probably just skulks around in the background, making sure his dues are paid and his Captains are behaving.

"Then yes, I want cookies," Lola grins. She thinks cookies made with the cannabutter taste funky and she has a point. But cookies are quick and easy to make, whereas decent brownies take time, they need to cool down to get that soft gooey center.

"What's your plan for Asaro now? I think you like him," she teases in a sing-song voice, blonde curls bouncing as she gives me a little shimmy.

She was much prettier than the other 'Flowers' at The Top Hat, and she worked hard, learning new dance routines all the time, taking care of her body. They didn't deserve her but at least she had the choice not to sell her body there, thanks to the new regulations Jay introduced. It was her business, her body and that's the way it should always be in this town for women like Lola and me. It's one of the reasons I'd been able to garner support from others in The Family, I wanted to protect them and I would do anything to ensure they were safe. Julian Asaro was losing men every year, admittedly...it was my fault. But if he'd had the balls and the ability to stop me, then he should, otherwise he was just another weak leader with a soft spot for a pretty face.

"I think you like your stalker," I snap, tossing a dish towel at her head.

She glances backwards at the window, now partially covered up, the outline of her artistic cock rendering shining through thanks to the street lighting. "He tips well, keeps his hands to himself and makes eye contact instead of staring at my tits. Of course I like him."

Men like that were usually too good to be true, especially to the dancer in The Top Hat. "Are you sure he's not dangerous?"

She flashes me a smug expression. "Oh, he's dangerous, Ro. But so am I."

We laugh but I feel more settled about it when we finally come to portioning out the cookie dough mix on a baking tray. Lola wasn't some airhead stripper, and sometimes I had to remind myself of that. She was the one who taught me how to survive on the streets, how to build a life with the scraps we managed to pull together and nothing but our brains. She also wasn't afraid to get her hands dirty, and in return for her taking me in, I'd shown her how to handle a knife and a gun like my father had taught me. You wouldn't want to meet either of us in a dark alley, and yet because of the hair and cute smiles, we were always underestimated.

"Are you really going to kill him?" she asks, voice quieter now. Concerned.

No.

Yes.

His life was mine. He owed me, and I wasn't about to write that debt off. He could have warned me. Could have warned them. We could have run together. Instead, he knew and he kept his mouth shut. No, worse than that. He put his mouth on mine, and made me want things I could never have. He turned me inside out, before hanging me out to dry. And that was unforgivable.

I turn my back on her so she can't see the hesitation that still lingers and I switch on her oven with a click. "Eventually."

A heavy bass thrums through my veins, as the crowds of people around me move to the beat. Swaying to a song I don't recognize, losing themselves to the moment to the feeling of being alive. I'd come to The Blue Caterpillar tonight with Lola, but she'd quickly vanished into a dark corner somewhere, no doubt seducing some poor, pretty schmuck.

I hadn't been here before, but I was enjoying the vibe. The crowd was young, eager, hungry for a good time and dancing always made me feel energized, like I could do anything.

Weaving through the sweaty bodies, I make my way to the bar and pull myself up onto a navy and gold stool. Dark glossy tiles and huge mirrors behind the bar, make it feel intimate, like an enclosed space where you could just curl up and hide, almost like a cocoon. Gold cages, with beautiful glittering blue butterflies hang just above my head, casting a dim light below.

Once I've ordered an Un-Birthday cocktail, a

curious concoction with rose liquor and pink fizz, I settle myself in one of the seating areas. Here the walls were a dark, deep navy color with a gradient that gradually fed into white at the top. The sofas were covered in velvet navy and white cushions, adorned with gold embroidery and tassels. It was all tastefully done, and I wasn't surprised given that it was owned by the Volkov twins, former Russian model socialites, turned business owners.

A few minutes later I'm joined by Cato, the designated dealer for this club. Tonight their dyed green hair is worn long around their shoulders, held back from their face with cute black glittery butterfly clips. Cato's rocking a black leather harness over a black mesh shirt, pierced nipples shining every time they catch in the lights. The same goes for their lip ring. This is teamed with a short-pleated shirt and a pair of thigh high-laced up boots. They look incredible, and for a moment I'm jealous. Tonight, I'd come out wearing an outfit I'd borrowed from Lola, a cute baby-doll mini dress in white with a tiny red heart pattern and a pair of red platform heels. I was adorable and fuckable in a bratty kind of way while Cato just looked sinful.

Cato leans forward, pulling me into a kiss as their hand links with mine. Up this close, I can see the gemstones they've placed around their eyes and the glitter that shimmers on their skin. When they finally pull away, my hand clenches around the small baggie they've left behind.

They offer me a small smile as they stroke my hair, curling it between their long slender fingers. "I've missed you Ro."

Cato was another one I'd met on the streets of East Point, where they'd been selling themselves for a pimp who didn't give a shit about his clientele. Lola and I kind of adopted Cato into our little found family, and for a while it was just the three of us. Cato eventually decided to move on, and there were no hard feelings about that. In fact, when they heard Lola had started working at The Top Hat, they'd reached out, desperate to reconnect. That was almost four years ago and now Cato was a Family approved drug dealer, which meant they were a valuable asset since dealers always had their ears to the ground. If anything happened in this town, Cato knew about it.

"What's this?" Grinning, I tuck the packet into my cleavage to inspect later.

They reach over and take a sip of my drink, using it as an excuse to get closer to me. Mouth inches away from my ear, they explain, "White Rabbit, it's new.

Cleaner apparently, less risky, not mixed with any nasty shit."

I doubt anyone can hear us over the music, but it never hurts to be cautious, so I slide my hands into their hair. Besides, it wasn't like it was a hardship to press myself against Cato. "Hmmmmm, and let me guess, twice the price?"

"No, actually." Hands roam up my legs, and to the outside world we look like two young people about to hook up in a club. "My sources say The Family has an agreement with an organization in Bolivia, meaning they control the regulation, the import and the price."

"Why would they do that?" I murmur, more for myself than Cato.

Kissing along the curve of my neck, Cato's words flutter across my skin. "There's always going to be drugs, that's a fact of life. Why not control what you can if you can?"

Tilting my head back, I laugh. "So, what, Julian Asaro is some sort of coke angel?"

Their hands slide under my skirt and dig into my ass as I'm pulled into their lap. "It's a power play. Control the drugs, control the quality and you'll control the people who buy it and sell it."

"Ahhhhh Cato, but my plan is to control the man who controls the drugs." I shimmy down their legs until I'm back, standing on my feet. "I want what's his. And I'm going to take it, one way or another."

Holding out my hand, I drag them back on to the dance floor, my mind filled with images of Julian Asaro's face when he discovers just how deep my roots run in this little Family tree.

Chapter Five

Julian

This day has been beyond hectic with two cases in court and a third giving me a headache with the inaccuracies of my client's alibi. Some days I hate working for rich assholes, because they always assumed I would be on their side, that I'd turn a blind eye to their lies, their money somehow rendering me into a clueless idiot when it came to their half-truths. Composing a quick email, I forward Eli the client's details for further investigation, hoping that The Family could find a valid reason to take care of him. I didn't trust Malcom Radcliffe as far as I could throw him, slimy motherfucker and I'd sleep much happier at night knowing that disgusting human was off my streets.

Not only did I have that to contend with, but now I have to go for dinner with a potential client when all I want is a good sweaty session in the gym and to get in some swimming afterwards. Fitness and taking care of my body had been drilled into me at a young age, my father adamant that I not be 'weak' or a 'sissy pushover'. With every lap of the park or painful sit-up I'd cursed him silently inside my head, wishing him a painful death for the life he made my mother and I live. Now exercise was one of my addictions. I needed the burn of my muscles, the ache distracting me from the million responsibilities weighing on my shoulders. It also helped keep my sweet tooth in check, another addiction. This one my father hadn't been able to beat out of me, despite his best efforts.

It's not that I don't love my job, because I do, being a lawyer was the only choice I'd gotten to make in my whole life, but everything was intense right now. Belcastro left The Family in a mess, with in-fighting, depleted resources and still stuck in the dark ages. I want to break it down and meld it into some-thing new, something stronger but resistance is making that difficult and then add in a high-pressured day job. I was like pasta dough, being pulled too thinly in too many directions.

All eight of my Captains were useful in their own ways, but promoting unity and bringing The Family out of the 'old ways' was still proving difficult. I didn't blame them, not really. The mafia was an organization built around family, trust and tradition and I was attempting to shake that up. Given that half of my Captains had been my father's before mine, I knew I was fighting an uphill struggle before I'd even begun. Thankfully, some of the younger ones like Matty Jr, Zeno and Nicco were less resistant to change, and understood the necessity of moving into the twenty-first century.

Family dynamics could wait, first dinner and schmoozing. I was lucky, in that I owned my own firm, started with the support of The Family and grown through my own hard work, allowing me to pace myself a little more and yet...and yet I still don't get the freedom to go for a fucking swim when I want. I inhale slowly, count to five and exhale with a deep sigh.

"And who is my dinner with?" I ask Daniel as I get into the car and loosen my tie.

"A potential client," he says, checking the watch I'd gifted him for his birthday as he climbs in beside me. It's unlike him to be vague but he seems on edge this evening as we drive downtown.

I open a bottle of water and chug down half of it, preparing my liver for what's about to come. Many of my clients liked to indulge at these meetings, since they were usually at my expense and it would be rude if I didn't share a drink. I'm not much of a drinker typically, I find alcohol gives me a headache and I can't think straight. Last week at the charity gala I'd indulged more than I usually would, and where had that gotten me? Dancing with my enemy, inhaling her ridiculously sweet scent as I held her close to my chest. It had come back to bite me, literally. Reaching up to stroke my ear, which was now healed, I flinch.

"And what's the case?"

Daniel shrugs. "They said they wanted to discuss it privately with you. I think it's something to do with property rights and fraud."

"Hmmm." I don't like the sound of this client already, they seem demanding.

"There will be two bodyguards outside at all times," Daniel reassures me with quiet confidence. I don't usually require bodyguards to tail my every move, but Elijah is away on a reconnaissance mission for me trying to hunt down Rosie once again while looking into some murmurings about a Mexican cartel trying to move in on my turf.

I haven't heard anything from Rosalyn Gambino since the gala and it unnerved me for some reason. It wasn't strange in itself, as I only hear from her on the anniversary of her parents' deaths normally. She commits her little acts of violence, posts me my gifts and fades back into the shadows but this time she'd approached me in public and I was hoping to get a lead on her before she vanished for another ten years.

After that night, when she'd fled and my father and Belcastro had forced her to go into hiding, I often wondered how she'd lived. How she'd survived, alone without a dollar to her name and with The Family hunting her down. I had my suspicions that she'd left Newtown completely, hiding out somewhere else for a few years and my theory seemed to fit with the time-line as the first hearts didn't begin arriving until three years after, on her twenty-first birthday. It took my father a while to realize who was behind the gift that had shown up at our home, addressed to me but once he did, it brought up all his anger again. He'd broken three of my ribs that night, said I deserved it for not handling the 'Gambino bitch', like I'd been told to. I push down the unpleasant memories resurfacing, cursing Rosie for stirring up my life once again.

"Fine." I scroll through my phone and see there's been another dead body washed up along the riverbank. I wonder who pissed off Lawrence again as I skim the police report. It looked like his style of kill; throat cut with multiple poker burns littering the victim's body. My Captain was very lucky we had an excellent relationship with Newtown PD. That and I had deep pockets. Turning my attention to Daniel, I ask, "Will you be joining us?"

He shifts in his seat, and glances out the window nervously. "I have that hospital appointment with my mother, Sir."

His mother. She was in a nursing home with dementia and with his father dead, it fell to Daniel to take care of her. I seemed to recall they were currently investigating some suspected frontal lobe damage, which must be difficult for my soft assistant. "Ah, I forgot. Okay, I'll see you in the office tomorrow then."

He doesn't reply, just nods. Talking about his family always makes Daniel clam up and I'm not entirely sure why. I mean, it was common knowledge, even outside The Family that my father was a tyrant. He'd been too tight with his affection and too liberal with his anger, and my mother had suffered the most. By the time she died half of her face was paralyzed from nerve damage and she walked with a limp, something that was often speculated about in gossip rags. I wasn't strong enough back then; I hadn't been able to do what needed to be done. He'd been a Captain for Frank Belcastro but Felix Asaro had always had bigger plans and he had no qualms when it came to getting what he wanted. So, if anyone has any reason to be ashamed of their parents, it's me. I came from a monster. And I too became a monster.

We pull up outside an expensive restaurant I've visited a few times where they do the most incredible chocolate mousse, so maybe tonight isn't a complete write off I think with a small smile. Getting out of the car I watch as it drives off to take Daniel to the hospital and after straightening my tie once again, I put on my lawyer face, a charming smile and enter the fancy venue with my black bank card burning a hole in my wallet.

I'm shown to a private room in the back, and as promised two bodyguards nod as I enter.

As a lawyer I often meet unsavory, desperate people.

As a wealthy man from a prominent family, I meet false, lecherous people.

And as the head of The Family, I meet greedy, homicidal people...like the one sat before me wearing a fitted white dress with bold red lipstick.

"Well, are you just going to stare?" she asks, pouring two glasses of red wine gracefully. For a moment, I wonder if poison is how I die. It would figure, since our relationship is already toxic. Intoxicating.

Without the mask hiding half of her face, I can see her clearly now. She looks older, the softness of her youth a little faded around the edges but she's still beautiful. Still deadly. Her dress hugs her curvy frame, and for a moment I think about how she's the image of her mother. My chest tightens with guilt, that I swallow as I step closer. Her blonde curls are delicately pinned up with an oriental hairpin, a ruby flower catching the candlelight every time she moves.

Raising my eyebrow, I look down at her. "What's going on? Are you here to kill me, because I warn you, I have men outside."

Not that they would be much help. We both knew she could do some serious damage before they even opened the door. She wasn't just a pretty face, and she wasn't called the Queen of Hearts for nothing.

"Do you now?" She flashes me a sneaky smile, and my stomach sinks. "Because I'm pretty sure only one is actually yours, Jay."

Great. If I call out or cause a commotion now, her man will deal with mine before he even sees the betrayal coming. And if they successfully manage to take each other out, or my bodyguard disarms hers, I'll still be left with the Queen of Hearts and I'm not a fool, I know she's better in close quarters than me. She was trained from birth for this role, something my father had always admired despite how much he hated Vincent Gambino.

"It's Julian," I correct with a fake smile, fixing my lawyer person in place as I cross my arms. Patience is a virtue; one I was very adept at. I just need to wait, bide my time and see what game she's playing. Once I figured out what her angle was, what she planned to do, then I could tug on the threads of her little scheme and watch her unravel.

"That's funny, that's not how you introduced yourself all those years ago." Tilting her head, her big baby blue eyes watching me carefully she retorts, "You also didn't seem to mind it at the gala."

"We were kids, Rosie. And you caught me off guard at the gala." I wait, watching as she tucks a glossy blonde curl behind her ear. Why did she have to be so attractive? When I read the reports of her crimes, or saw the troubles she was causing in the lower ranks I always tried to imagine her as this plain-looking woman, twisted with hatred but she was flawless, like a Venus flytrap, drawing me in and I hated it. I hated my reaction to her. I'd almost invited her home with me at the gala, and if she hadn't told me who she was, she might have been naked in my bed that night.

"Rosalyn then." Her eyes sparkle as she takes a sip of her wine; she's enjoying this too much. She's plotting something.

Holding up my hands in defeat I growl, "Fine. Be infuriating."

"Sit," Rosie commands, but I hesitate. "Sit. If I wanted you dead, you already would be."

"I know." As much as it pains me, she's right. She could have killed me multiple times over the last ten years. She could have killed me the night of the raid on her house or last week at the gala. I, unlike her, was someone of a sitting duck with my public persona and my active roles in Newtown. All it would take was a well-timed bomb, a talented sniper or a staged mugging gone wrong. If I wasn't at the top of her list, and if she wasn't so desperate to get her hands on me herself, I would already be six feet under and she'd be sitting on top of my grave, on her throne, wearing the crown she'd stolen from me.

I bite the inside of my cheek as I take the seat opposite her. Sliding the glass of wine she poured closer, I ran my thumb up and down the stem as I tried to weigh out my options.

She flashes me another dangerous smile. "Exactly, so why play games?"

Despite my earlier resolution to not drink too much too quickly, I swallow the wine in two large gulps. I assume that it must be safe, since she's drinking it too. "I thought this was all just a big game to you?"

She shrugs, as she stands. "No. It's about revenge. It's about reparations."

"So, you aren't enjoying yourself?" I scoff, with a frown as she reaches across me to pour another drink. Rosie took too much pride in her 'gifts', in the carcasses she left behind for it to be solely about revenge.

Placing the bottle down she moves away but I grab her wrist and hold her in place, leaning close to her. Her skin is soft and warm beneath my hand, and there it is again, cherries and cinnamon. She watches me carefully, and this close I can see the flecks of gold and grey in her eyes, the thick long lashes framing her larger eyes, the steady swipe of eyeliner on her eyelid. She's a carefully constructed honey trap, and my mouth goes dry as I wonder about how that would taste in the moments before the inevitable betrayal.

"I enjoy getting a rise out of you," she whispers, angling closer until her words skim against the shell of my ear. "But I wouldn't exactly describe my gifts as fun..."

"Then stop."

She chuckles softly, her breath tickling the skin on my neck and I swallow a groan. "I will, when everyone has paid their debt."

"When I'm dead then," I say calmer than I feel. It's not like I didn't know what awaited me. I've known it every day for the last ten years. I've lived with that knowledge, carried it around like a rock in my pocket, trying to ignore the way it weighed me down. "I'm your end goal Rosie, let's not pretend otherwise."

"I'm saving you for last. I want to savor every moment. Every touch. Every scream." With the last word, Rosie nips my earlobe and I resist the urge to lean into her despite her track record with my appendages. The scar on my hand tingles as I tighten my grip on her wrist. Why did she make death sound positively carnal? "You are mine."

"I know," I murmur. I have always known it. It's the reason I can't kill her. The reason I wait, and watch. I tell myself it's because I'm a fair leader and I want to give her the chance to repent, to return to The Family but somewhere deep down I know it's because the more I learn about Rosie Gambino, the more I want. The more she intrigues me. "Both of our lives changed that night."

"You became a Prince, Julian. Then you became a King. Don't act like you know what I went through." There's an edge to her voice, and I know I've hit a soft spot. If I put pressure on it, she'll cut my throat without even blinking, plan be damned. Everything else is fun and games, but not the bitterness lurking beneath the surface.

Needing to deescalate the anger I can feel festering, I pull her a little closer so we're practically cheek to cheek. "You were always supposed to be mine."

"I was supposed to be a Queen." The words sound hollow, and it takes me straight back to that night. To the girl in the pretty dress, sitting on the bench looking lost. To the star-gazers who knew nothing about the real world and what waited for them. "Nothing else mattered. Our marriage was an unwanted side effect."

"It didn't need to be. We could have been partners." I trace small lazy circles on the inside of the wrist, offering her comfort, reassuring her that there doesn't have to be bloodshed between us.

The corner of her mouth tugs up into a slow smile and I flinch. It's cruel. It's another mask, a wall she's putting up to keep me out. "I've always been aware of my place, Julian. And it was never under you."

Except it could be. And on top. And beside me.

What was I doing? I need to stop her, not fuck her.

"Empty. That was your life Rosie, you said it yourself," I remind her gently, trying to reach the young girl I know is still buried deep down inside. "And now?"

She flicks her tongue over my skin, making me shiver. "Angry."

Chapter Six

Rosie

C an you hate-fuck someone you want to kill? Is that a thing? Because Julian Asaro is pushing all of my buttons right now. And he smells incredible. He smells like saltwater and mint, a masculine margarita and I'm desperate for a drink. The urge to lick his neck, follow the line of his body and bite into his Adam's apple, marking him as mine is like some base compulsion I can't even explain.

"Anger is good. But I can think of better ways to express it than murder." Of course Saint Julian has alternative outlets for my destructive rage, all no doubt benefiting The Family. But I'm not like him, I don't require their approval. I don't have to peace-keep between old crusty-men who haven't seemed to realize that the world has moved on. Violence is the only language they understand, it's the only reason they fear me and I refuse to temper that and pack it away in a little pink box so Julian Asaro can make me more palatable for his Captains.

"So can I." There are so many things I could do to Julian. Pleasure and pain are a deadly combination, and there's a very fine line between the two. One I relish. One I crave. I know he recognizes it too, his pupils widening as he tilts his head back and inhales slowly.

"Get your mind out of the gutter Rosie, before we do something you'll regret." His voice was huskier now.

I know he can feel it, whatever this pull between us is. It's toxic. It's history and memories that hurt. It's the things that should have been, and the things we'll never have. It's rage and retribution, twisted together until it consumes us. I can feel my fingers practically twitch at the thought of loosening his tie and showing him just how angry I was. I wanted to mark him, to scar him, to ruin him for everyone and everything that comes after.

"And what's that?" I tease, knowing he wants me

the same way I want him, with claws and teeth. He tugs on my wrist harder, twisting me so I fall into his lap. Both of his arms wrap around me like a vice holding me in position, not that I'd fight him anyway. Not when things were finally getting interesting.

"You're going to get burned, little girl."

I look up at him, and his serious face, emerald eyes watching me with an intensity that makes my thighs clench together. I've followed him over the years, kept track of his life through social media, the news, and my contacts. He was just as gorgeous now as he was then, before he'd grown into his tall frame and strong features. His blond hair had darkened a little, but still made him look angelic. His jawline spots a little stubble and the woman in me wants to rub my cheek against it, while the Queen of Hearts wants to follow it down his neck and strangle him. He is always so serious and somber, like he has the weight of the world on his shoulders. Some days I'd watched from afar, wanting to shake him. He was living my life, and it wasn't even making him happy. If he didn't want to be the head of The Family, he could always just hand me the organization.

"I'm not a child Jay, I think I can take it." Reassuring him, as I squirm in his lap a little. I can see him wrestling with himself, even though his expression remains calm. He's collected on the outside, but I recognize the hunger in his eyes.

"You're the Queen of Hearts," he states, gaze locked with mine.

"Yes." The word is slow and drawn out as I tilt my head. Where is this going? There's no judgement in his voice, there never has been when he calls me that. He knows who I am and what I've done. He knows why and a part of him has accepted that. He still wants to stop me, but that's because he has to. I'm a threat to him and the tenuous hold he has on all the strings behind The Family.

I used to listen to him give interviews about some of his clients in the media and he was always so cool, so relaxed and unruffled about everything. Julian was a man who took everything in his stride, apparently, even his arch enemy squirming in his lap like a bitch in heat.

"You're trying to ruin my organization..." He inches closer and tucks a hand under my chin. Looking at me carefully, his eyes narrow, like I'm one of his cases and he's trying to figure out just how to approach me. How to win me over, so that I vanish once again.

"Yeah." My lips twitch as I arched a brow. Grateful that I'd chosen this restaurant, I admire the golden glows the candles sconces cast across his face, adding to the intimacy that I've only ever felt with him. I commit this moment to memory, because it's real. It's not one I've stolen from a news clipping or recorded from an interview. It's real, and it's ours.

"Kill my men..." He tilts my chin upwards so that our noses are almost touching. I can feel his breath on my skin, sending shivers down my spine as I breathe in the rich notes of the wine lingering between us. I would forever associate this wine with him, with this almost kiss.

"Only certain ones," I say with a grin, the thrill of finally being this close to him beginning to go to my head. The boy who saw everything all those years ago, the same one who stole everything was close enough for me to devour, and he wasn't even flinching.

He groans, the noise delicious. "So why are you under my skin?"

"Because I'm poison." I brush my lips against his, with every word. I needed to hear him acknowledge the tension between us, the destructive bond binding us together and he did. This is more than hate. And nothing like love. It's death and lust. It's inevitable.

"Fuck," he moans on an exhale. His large hand shifts up my neck, strong thick fingers weaving their way into my hair as he yanks my head backwards.

Forcing me to stay in position, we stare at each other, locked in a moment there are no words for before his mouth crashes against mine.

It isn't sweet or slow, it's desperate. Teeth clashing, tongues fighting for dominance as we consume one another. It's like every nerve in my body wakes up, screaming for attention as I try to savor every touch, every sensation. Sliding my hands over his shoulders, I pull him deeper into me. It's not enough. It will never be enough. He tastes bittersweet, like everything I should have had, but never can. Like broken promises and potential. How can a kiss taste like potential?

I can't help the soft mewling noises that are torn from my throat as his tongue does things I've only ever fantasized about, all the while pulling at me like he's afraid I'm sand, slipping through his fingers. Our connection has a time limit. It has an end. One of us will cut the cord, and we both know it.

He lifts me, never pulling away, his lips still on mine as he puts me on the table, pushing the glasses and cutlery away without a second thought. Everything lands with a crash, plates smashing and crockery clinking and clattering. None of it matters.

Spreading my legs, and placing himself between them, he pushes my dress up my thighs slowly. Hands massage my thighs as he keeps kissing me, mouth touching any part of my skin he can. He nuzzles my neck, biting and licking before moving lower, reaching the lines of my collarbone before moving back to my mouth.

Taking his lead I wrap my legs around his waist, grinding against him with an impatient moan. One hand rests on my back, holding me in position, while the other roams over my body as if he's mapping me out.

He pulls away to kiss my shoulders, sliding the straps of my dress down and pulling the fabric beneath my bra. He uses the space between us to remove his jacket and toss it behind him. His touch is impatient, like he's been waiting his whole life to touch me and I love it. Nothing makes a woman feel sexier, than a man who wants to touch every curve of her body like she's made from gold.

Growing restless, I grab his tie and pull it from him before working on his buttons. As my hands make quick work of his shirt, dropping it carelessly to the floor, my fingers brush against the hard muscle of his chest. He was a machine beneath the suit, something people seemed to forget even though he'd been voted 'Newtown's Hottest Batchelor' the last three years in a row. I knew he swam and worked out with his Left

Hand, Creed, almost daily. What I wouldn't give to see those two, hot and sweaty, lifting weights like they were nothing. It was total girl porn. I skim my fingers down the lines either side of his hips, the ones that make the mouth-watering V shape, before I undo the button on his trousers, loving how he shifts, offering me more of his body. I slide my hands down, and cup his dick over his boxers. I squeeze, loving the feel of him against my palm. Kissing him harder, as I eventually remove my hand, I use my nails to lightly trace up the length of his cock, getting a thrill as it twitches. Looking at his muscular physique beneath my hands I'm not sure I could take him on in a one-to-one situation. He was sneaky like that.

Julian played down his training regime publicly and even my inside sources were unsure where his specialties lay outside of the gym. He could be just as talented as me with a blade, however my gut instinct said he was more of a gun person. Something long range, where he could watch and wait. He also would be trained in hand-to-hand; Felix Asaro would have insisted upon it.

His fingers trail their way up my thigh, eliciting a soft sigh from me as I claim his mouth once again. It was a shame this wouldn't last. It couldn't. Hitching my leg upwards, he positions me so that my heels are resting on the table and I'm spread open for him, palms resting behind me to support myself.

I arch into him as he brushes against the lace of my panties. I'm so wet right now that he must be able to feel it as he teases me through the material. Fingers applying pressure to the right spot as he pushes my knees with his other hand. The burn, the stretch in my thighs being spread wide apart drags another groan from my lips.

"Fucking knew it . . ." He groans against my neck and I'm desperate for more. More of his kisses. More of his touch. More of him. Julian Asaro was my vice. Just as he's about to remove the only barrier between us, he pauses with a frown. Stumbling backwards, mouth twisted as his pupils narrow, I know our fun has come to an end.

Chapter Seven

Julian

I've waited for ten years to taste Rosie, to touch her like this, to own her. She's been the thorn in my side, and a constant reminder of everything we should have had. She was always supposed to be mine, like this. The scent of cherries is strongest on her neck, like she's been rubbing it with cherry juices still on her fingertips and it drives me wild. I keep burying my face against her skin, needing more. If I could subsume her, keep her like this, I would even, though I can hear Eli's warnings rattling around my head. She's dangerous but I can't seem to stop myself.

It's surreal as she offers herself up to me willingly, giving me everything I wanted with no resistance.

Encouraging it, moaning as I rub against her damp underwear. Kissing me like I'm the air she needs to breathe. She wants me. There's no denying that. No doubt of the attraction between us. It's always been there since we were teenagers in that damn garden. That spark was now a roaring flame as my hands followed every line and curve of her body. She's on the table like the finest dessert, spread wide for me, eager and waiting.

But does she want me enough?

Is it enough to put an end to her vendetta? To come back to The Family and be by my side? Could we even have that? Would the others accept her?

I was getting ahead of myself, those were problems we could discuss later, when we were naked and tangled up in one another. Right now, I just wanted to be buried inside her, to consume her, to hear her moan my name while she rode my dick like she was a jockey at the fucking Kentucky Derby. I wanted Rosie Gambino like I'd never wanted anyone else and it was burning me alive.

My fingertips brush against the lace of her underwear again, and as I'm about to slide my hand inside and feel that slickness for myself, a wave of nausea washes over me. My stomach clenches. I feel wrong. Slow. My head feels fuzzy, and my mouth is suddenly dry as I try to get my words out. Everything is hazy, blurry around the edges as I step back from Rosie.

I open my mouth to say something, to reassure her, but when I see her pull up her dress to cover her tits, and she crosses her legs elegantly as she perches on the edge of the table, skirt pulled back down in place, I know. This is undoubtedly her doing.

"Whaaa . . ." I groan as I fall back into my chair, my body heavy and cumbersome. It was like I could no longer support myself, I felt exhausted. It's like she's a succubus, draining the life from me as it becomes effort to even think.

"I'm sorry Jay, I was having so much fun." She pouts a little, as she straightens her hair. "But I can't trust you to let me leave and I have somewhere else to be tonight."

She didn't trust me? My brain might be turning to mush, but the irony of the situation wasn't lost on me. She'd lured me down here, removed half of my clothes and then poisoned me. Yet I was the one who couldn't be trusted?

"H-ooo-w?" I manage to rasp out as my limbs ache. I can't even lift my hand as I sink back into my chair.

"I didn't put anything in the wine, I knew you'd suspect that." She shrugs, looking around at the mess we'd made. Smashed glass and discarded cutlery littered the floor, the red wine had spilled, creating a blood-red puddle on the hardwood floor. "It was my lipstick."

Of course it was. She was a Venus flytrap. Enticing and deadly. I knew that and yet I still kissed her, I still held her like she was mine. Did that mean she only kissed me to kill me? Was that her plan all along? No, she wanted this as much as I did. I felt it.

Her shoulders droop a little as she stands, brushing her hands down over her dress as if she was trying to smooth out the creases. "I told you I was poison. I warned you, I've been warning you for years."

She did. I knew not to trust her, and yet for some reason I thought...I thought the chemistry between us might have been enough to convince her to change her mind. I should have known better, Rosie never trusted anyone. She wouldn't listen to me that night and not in the aftermath. I blamed her father for that, for her deep suspicion of everyone. For all the love Vincent Gambino had shown his wife and daughter, he'd never taught them how to trust anyone else. He kept them cloistered away in their giant home in the suburbs, with the sprawling rose gardens and endless rooms. He made sure they were separate from The Family, never mingling with anyone outside of Vincent's circle unless they had to. He taught her to be a weapon and a woman, both dangerous.

Was my irrational trust in a woman I barely knew but felt like I'd known my whole life about to get me killed? Probably. It was a highly likely outcome given how I could no longer feel my fingers or toes.

It's like she can read my mind as she grabs her purse and explains, "It won't actually kill you, it's just to buy me some time to leave."

And humiliate me, since someone will find me like this. Word will get back to my Captains, filtering down to the others and once again, Rosalyn Gambino will have made a mockery of me and my position within The Family.

"Why?" I croak, my throat on fire as I force the word out.

She pulls red rope from her purse, and quickly sets to work fastening me to the chair. Looping and knotting the cord across my chest, binding my hands until I have no hope of moving, even if I was able to. Standing back to admire her handiwork, a flash of desire lights up her gaze and I wonder if she'd done this before. Glancing away, she bends down and scoops something up off the floor.

"I can't be here...I'm supposed to stay in the shadows," she offers up, clutching my tie.

It wasn't time, that was the unspoken truth. There were still others on her list, still names that had to be crossed off before she was supposed to approach me. She was breaking her own rules by seeking me out and it was jeopardizing her entire plan.

Silence fills the room before she takes a deep breath and flashes a big smile at me. It's fake, the smile. It doesn't reach her eyes as she looks me over once more. "I think I should take my leave Jay."

"W—aaait." I can't believe she's doing this to me. When I'm able to move again, I'm going to wring her goddamn gorgeous neck. I'm going to chain her up so she can never run away again. I can't move at all now and it feels like I'm sitting in a block of concrete as my chest gets tight, my breathing ragged and rough as I attempt to suck in more air. Panic starts building in my chest, and I don't believe her earlier words that she isn't trying to kill me off just yet.

"Breathe, Jay, it will feel uncomfortable. But I promise you, you're not dying." Her fingers brush against my cheek as she attempts to reassure me. Her hand drifts up to my hair, where she plays with it for a few moments, running it through her fingers.

I stare at the tie; she's still clasping it and I have no idea why.

"Oh, I'm keeping this." She frowns, withdrawing her hand and ending our contact. "Hmmm, it doesn't seem polite to take something of yours without giving you something in return."

If I could move, I'd snort. Rosie didn't give a damn about manners or being polite. I know she's waiting to make sure that the toxins are fully in my system, I can tell by the way she keeps checking the clock above the door behind me. Always meticulous. Always calculating.

My lips are no longer my own as they refuse to move. I can't even groan out an attempt at a word anymore, my whole body rebelling thanks to her. Making a mental note to never underestimate her again, I try to calm my breathing.

She pulls out her compact and reapplies her deadly lipstick. The red brings out her pronounced cupid's bow and the fullness of her bottom lip. "Oh. Wait, I have it."

I watch, my brain foggy as she slips a hand up her dress and shimmies out of her underwear. With a grin, she tucks them between my lips, carefully checking that I can still breathe. "Until we meet again."

Planting a kiss on my cheek she sashays away. I'm left, paralyzed by the whirlwind that is Rosalyn, tied to a chair with damp panties, still smelling like her, shoved in to my mouth.

***

"She did what to you?" Elijah tries to hide his laugh but fails as he sits in my living room, drinking beer and eating pizza. His long dark hair is tied half-up with a messy bun, the rest falling down past his shoulders. He looks relaxed and at home, in his grey sweats and a tight black T-shirt.

I was still wearing my suit from another hectic day at the office, I'd barely stepped through the door of the large house I'd bought on the outskirts of the city and removed my tie before Eli had thrust a cold beer into my hand and slapped my back with a wide grin.

Elijah Creed is more than just my Left Hand, the man who enforces my rules and cleans shit up when plans go wrong. He is my friend. We'd met when we were just ten years old, our fathers both Captains under Belcastro. Mine was responsible for managing The Gryphon and several businesses up-town, while Eli's father oversaw drug warehouses downtown, in the shadier part of Newtown. They were working a job together, another one of Belcastro's witch hunts for people allegedly stealing money from him and we'd been forced to watch the interrogation as part of our 'education'.

He was another kid who grew up in a fucked-up situation, with a drug addicted mother, a vindictive, cruel father and now he can't do anything else but fall into this life. It's all we know. It's the only place we feel like we can survive and that's why we call it Family.

"Yep," I swig my bottle of beer. "My bodyguard had to come and help me home. And I still can't get this damn red off my cheek."

I glance in the mirror behind Eli, where her lipstick mark was still visible on my cheek. It had barely faded, although I had scrubbed and scrubbed, but it was like Lady Macbeth's damned spot. A symbol of my guilt, of my stupidity in trusting a Gambino when I should have known better. It wasn't enough that the woman tricked me, poisoned me, left me half-naked and unsatisfied but she had the audacity to mark me too? I had to hide in my office all day to avoid anyone seeing it while I was at work. It wouldn't happen again. I couldn't afford another slip-up like that one, not when I was responsible for making sure The Family ran as it should.

"So, what was she like?" Elijah asks from my armchair as he tucks into another slice of meat feast pizza. "You said you didn't really talk much at the gala, but last night you were there for a while..."

"Fucking crazy. Certifiable," I groan, as I lean back on the sofa. I don't have the words to describe her, not in a way that would make sense. I hate her, but I also want to fuck her. I want to kill her, and ruin her life but I also feel guilty over our past and I want to make her happy. How was that even possible? What was wrong with me?

Between mouthfuls he waggled his eyebrows at me. "Crazy, as in freak in the sheets, or as likely to stab you for breathing the wrong way? Reckon she'd eat your heart?"

"You know that's just a rumor." I slide my hand into my pocket and touch the lace underwear she left behind. I don't know why I've been carrying her panties with me since yesterday, but I have. I laugh before polishing off my beer. "Both. At the same time, knowing her."

Fuck, wouldn't that be an insane way to die.

"And is she hot without the mask?" Eli ventures, watching me carefully. I hate it when he does this, morphing from my friend into my Left Hand seamlessly. He's assessing the risk; trying to work out what his next move should be and whether he needs to defy me to eliminate the threat. There is a reason I will never play chess with a man like Elijah Creed, and it's because I know I will always lose. He's the best at out-thinking his opponents. He's always five steps ahead and when he catches you, you never see it coming. He may be relaxed and easy with me, but I knew others found him intimidating and oddly quiet, but that was just him, waiting for monsters to jump out of the shadows at any moment.

I take another bottle off the coffee table and pop the cap, taking a mouthful and swallow slowly before I answer with a grin. "A ten. Easily."

"Well, there are worse ways to die." His voice hitches, and for a second, he sounds almost inter-ested. He shrugs, holding his hands up in defense when I fix him with a glare. "I'm just saying…"

"She's going to cause trouble again. I can feel it." I run a hand through my hair in frustration. How could she just leave like that? There's no way she'll be able to stay away, not now. Not knowing what the heat between us feels like. She won't be able to resist that for long, because I don't think I could.

"Then let me handle it." Creed sits back, head tilted as his dark eyes narrow. The logical part of my brain tells me that I should just let him. If he killed her, Lawrence and the others would stop pressuring me to do something about her. They'd quit bitching in my ear about how I was letting a woman make a mockery of me and our organization.

"She's mine," I mumble, aware that I sound a little bit like a spoiled child, unsure whether to be angry at what she did, or upset that she left. Could I be annoyed at both? Blue balls might kill me first, if Rosie doesn't and I don't know how to feel about that. Was it normal to lust after the person trying to kill you?

"And there's your problem, Jay," Elijah teases, before becoming more serious. "You're too attached. God knows why, I mean didn't you only meet her once before she showed up at the charity gala?"

Elijah didn't understand. His father hadn't cared about Family politics, Augustine was happy with the slice of pie Belcastro had given him and he defended it furiously. My father wanted seconds, and thirds, desperate to expand our influence and reach. I'd known about Rosie Gambino since the day she was born even though I never actually had a conversation with her until I was twenty-two. I'd seen her though, at Family events, heard about her from the soldiers and even some of the Captains had whispered about her as her skills grew.

Everyone knew about Rosie; they knew what her

father was grooming her for and that didn't sit well amongst the traditionalists. She was a threat to their way of life, their values and the very notion of Family. Vincent kept her away from the other high-ranking Family members, so that they couldn't influence her, keeping her sheltered. It wouldn't have mattered anyway, The Family hated anything they didn't understand, and a female leader came under that umbrella. They didn't invite her to events and gatherings unless all the Captains were expected to be in attendance, and that suited the Gambino's just fine.

A power that can't be influenced, bribed or threatened is a dangerous one and so they made a decision to cut her down before she had the chance to bloom, just like one of her mother's precious roses. If only they realized the part they played in creating the monster she was now, since that distance from The Family also allowed her to kill them without remorse.

My father had watched her progress with eagle eyes, noting every time Vincent made a kill that seemed unusual or out of place. He wanted to know what Rosie was becoming, and when our engagement was decided, I knew he was concerned about the arrangement since my father didn't believe I was 'man enough' to tame a wild woman like Rosie. He was right. In the garden, I hadn't been prepared for the reality of it. I hadn't been prepared for the beautiful girl, with the sad eyes and the gentle laugh. I certainly hadn't been ready for the warrior Queen, who slid her knife into my hand like I was nothing, not a living, breathing person but an obstacle.

"Everything changed that night. Everything," I mumble, reaching for the last slice of pizza.

Chapter Eight

Rosie

I sit back and watch as the others sitting around the table begin to argue amongst themselves. I cannot believe I left a half-naked, fully hard Julian Asaro tied to a chair for this. Naked hot man who was desperate for me, in exchange for a bunch of idiots who can't see farther than the noses on their faces. Rubbing my temple, I glance around the crowded room, taking in the faces of the people who were here tonight to support me.

The shouting and name-calling start quickly, voices getting louder and louder but I can't make myself play mediator tonight. I could have been having the best sex of my life, and I don't have any second guesses about it - it would have been incredible. And instead, I'm here. Not bitter about it, not bitter at all.

Grabbing the small gun out of my purse, I fire two warning shots into the ceiling without hesitation. Chunks of plaster land on the long table in front of me, but the mess is nothing new. The walls were covered in cracks and missing chunks, graffiti and faded posters barely covering up the rundown state of our meeting place.

"Are you done now, children?" I ask, clicking my tongue, sitting back and looking at all the stunned faces. Great, there was plaster dust on my dress.

Silence greets me.

"Good." I cross my arms and glare at all of them. "I am not going to hurt innocents to get a reaction out of Asaro and his supporters. That's not how this is going to go down."

Several people nod and others look annoyed but they bite their tongues. Our aim was to undermine Asaro's authority in The Family, not kill whoever we pleased just to create carnage. I'd spent too long plotting and planning my revenge to go off on some half-cocked killing spree that had no benefit for me.

I wasn't a bloodthirsty psycho; I was a considerate one.

A rat-faced man, with red cheeks and small beady eyes down the end of the table scoffs, "Don't tell me the Queen of Hearts is afraid of a little bloodshed?"

He chuckles bitterly as he crosses his arms, mimicking my pose as he looks to the others, trying to get them to join him as he grumbles about how I run my ship.

Squinting, I try to place him, but I don't recognize his face at all and yet he thinks he can taunt me. Rolling my eyes, with a bored sigh I take a small throwing knife from my garter. I'm grateful I thought to pack it in my purse, quickly sliding it up my leg in the cab over here from the restaurant. It's flying through the air and into the man's skull with a meaty noise before anyone even has a chance to blink.

I stand, slamming my hands down. "Bloodshed isn't the problem. The innocents are. And who the fuck was that guy anyway?"

"Paulie, are you bringing randoms in here now?" Everyone either avoids my glare or shrugs. "Don't we have a vetting process or something? A secret knock? A code word that excludes douchebags?"

Our monthly meetings were held in the cellar in one of Paulie Russo's strip clubs. He was an older man, gruff with a salt and pepper beard hiding a face that might have been handsome in his younger years. He was one of the good ones, who'd helped me because of his loyalty to my mother and the friendship they'd had when they were younger.

His clubs aren't the most glamorous, the music vibrates through the ceiling above us, and the venue is seedy and sticky but it provides an excellent cover for gunfire and heated arguments. Plus, it's another Family property, which is like sticking two fingers up at Julian as I plan to bring his kingdom down.

Paulie flips me off with a grin. He's one of the few that I can joke with since he understands my humor and doesn't think I'll carve out his heart to eat it. I sit back down with an exaggerated huff. "Just letting anyone in I fucking see."

"Rosalyn, we need to do something that will have Julian's followers questioning whether they're on the right side," a voice to my left fumes. I can barely make out faces with the crappy lighting down here, but I don't need to. I can hear the murmurs of agreement and know that this is causing ripples in my little rebellion.

"Everyone knows he's too soft, he won't retaliate. He'll let it slide," Esme, one of my Captains, remarks with a frown on her face. She's young, smart and very vocal about her unhappiness with how certain members of The Family are treated. "I mean, you murder his men and send him the hearts like a gift and he's still not reacted."

I am the exception. Julian doesn't let it slide like they assume; he's just playing the long game and they seem to forget that. I don't give him much of an option, since I refuse to stop. Besides, I think a small part of him accepts his role in what I do every year, his guilt is what keeps him from finding me.

Cassie, another of my Captains, an older woman whose husband is actually one of Julian's Captains, chimes in. "They'll think he's weak."

Her husband thinks she's at a knitting circle this evening, learning how to make scarves ready for the winter.

I raise my hand and silence the growing titters and mumblings. "And they'll think we're crazy and have no regard for life. That's not how we roll. Necessary sacrifices only, and not like this. Not to prove a point."

I don't even know how we got here, earlier this afternoon I was getting the sanity kissed out of me by the very man I was plotting to bring down. Now I was attempting to calm an angry mob of women and men marginalized in their own organization. In their own Family.

At the restaurant, I'd included the lipstick poison as a failsafe, a way to get out of there without him following me or trying to keep me as a prisoner. I had planned it so that if it got out of hand, I would still be in control, so why did I feel disappointed that we had to stop when we did? To top it off, I also felt more out of control than ever.

A nasal voice I recognize as belonging to Valentina Bruno, one of my more challenging supporters since her husband is Julian's Consigliere, intrudes upon my thoughts of Julian. "His leadership is tenuous; people want to go back to the old ways. They want power and glory, like the good old days."

Her words don't sit right with me, they sound just like her husband's and I can't believe the levels of stupidity in this room tonight. I didn't exactly trust my Captains, not the way I did Lola or even Cato, but there was no way to challenge Jay on my own. I needed support, and I needed it to be solid, otherwise it was worthless. The people in this room were the result of almost ten years of cultivated friendships, relying upon my parents' connections and recruiting the generation who knew that things needed to change.

"Excuse me?" Leaning forward to rest my elbows on the table, I look around. Some of them wriggle beneath my glare and others try to hide, sinking into the shadows. "Look around you. In the good old days, how many of you would have been sitting at this table?"

Silence once again as they look at each other. In my little rebellion, women had as much right to men to have a place at my table. Yep, that's how I garnered support in the aftermath of my parents' death.

I didn't go to the men in the organization for support, I went to their wives and their daughters. I went as an orphaned eighteen-year-old girl, who had everything ripped away by the patriarchal, outdated system we had in place. I played the gender card, and I reinforced the idea of family...actual family. Having one another's back and caring for each other. I reminded them that I had been chased out of Newtown, and I was risking everything by coming back to seek support.

They all knew who I was when I travelled into town from East Point and begged for their help—I'd been making their husbands nervous since I was eleven. My name spread through hushed whispers in the kitchens, in the baby and mother groups and at the bingo hall but they seemed to be forgetting what it was I was offering. I wasn't some sort of evil Queen unleashing my hatred on Newtown, I had very specific goals and desires and I was willing to do what it took to achieve them.

"Exactly. I've brought you to my table so that we can create something better. Not the same. I am not going backwards, and if you have a problem with that then you need to leave now." I wait.

Paulie opens the cellar door, but no one moves. Good. Because despite my brave words, I probably need them more than they need me right now.

"We do this my way and we do it right," I say. The rat-faced man's body is still slumped at my table, blood slowly trickling its way across the varnished wood. "Can someone please take this idiot out of here. He's ruining the vibe."

The rest of the meeting seems to go okay, but there's still a feeling of unease as I leave. They want results faster, and they're starting to not care about the methods any longer and that doesn't sit right with me. There still needs to be boundaries in place, otherwise the city would become feral.

"Well, that was intense." I laugh as I link my arm through Esme's as we make our way towards her apartment. I'm staying at her place tonight since I have business near her home tomorrow, and then I'll be at Lola's again for a few more nights.

"You're always intense Rosie," Esme chuckles as she pats my hand. We'd met not long after the attack on my house, Esme was another victim of that night.

Her father had been helping Felix, following orders like a good little soldier while his wife, Esme's mother, had been caught in the crossfire and lay dying in my hallway. She blamed her father for the death of her mother, it was unnecessary and violent. It could have been avoided if the entire situation had been handled differently, but that night was a stain on the memories for so many of us.

I sigh, knowing that some people saw me as bloodthirsty and reckless, not understanding that every move I made was carefully calculated to keep me off Julian's radar while gathering the support I needed for a coup. I had a plan . . . my father had taught me to always have a plan.

"I know you don't mean to be." She squeezes my arm, trying to reassure me. "I just don't think you realize how scary you can be."

Flashing her a sweet smile I pull her into a hug.

I know how frightening I am.

I know what I'm capable of.

I've always known.

A timer shrills, and I grab my pie dough from the fridge. Dusting Lola's tiny counter with flour, I drop the dough with a *thwop*, making Lola and Cato laugh as they sit on the loveseat and watch me. My yellow shorts and tank top pajamas are already covered in flour.

"Why have you decided to grace us with your presence tonight?" I ask, pointing my rolling pin in Cato's direction. They grin, and wave me off, their many bangles jingling as they do. Tonight, they look a little more masculine, wearing a black fitted T-shirt, ripped blue jeans and thick leather wrist cuffs. Their long hair is braided at the sides and pulled back into a messy bun.

Lola slaps their arm playfully, before pulling them into a hug. "Yeah, I thought it was risky to socialize with us too much."

Cato nuzzles Lola's shoulder. "I have gossip and I thought it might help your little vendetta."

I roll the dough, turn it and roll again. Repeating the process until I'm happy. Sliding my hands underneath, I carefully lift the sweet pastry sheet and line my pie tin. My cherry filling is already simmering away on the stove with so much sugar, I can feel my teeth ache, but that's how Lola likes it.

"Spill," Lola says, nudging Cato before offering them some chips out of the giant bag she's been nursing for the last hour. She's had an awful shift at work, and is currently drowning her sorrows in carbs, cheap white wine and her baggy-holey pajamas. Hence, the pie.

Taking a handful of the tortilla chips, Cato looks at both of us, eyes wide, mouth pursed as they say, "The Cartel have blocked the Bolivian imports. The Family are about to run into some serious trouble pushing White Rabbit until it's resolved."

That was Julian's current money-maker, and an attempt to clean up the streets in a manner of speaking. However, if there's no supply...there's no money. No money, no power. No control. His Captains would have something to say about this, probably condemning him for trying something new and then for being weak enough that another gang feels like they can encroach.

"The Mexican cartel?" Lola repeats, dunking her chips into the open tub of salsa next to her wine.

Cato does the same. "Yeah, except they're just calling themselves The Cartel."

I snort, so not only were they foolish for goading The Family, but they also lacked the originality to come up with something better for their gang's name.

They were wannabe's who were just looking to stir the pot.

"Brave of them to make moves like this, who've they got on the inside?" I ponder aloud as I pour the pie filling into the base and begin latticing the top. It's strange that they're finally making their move when there are waves within The Family, almost like they have insider knowledge. "There's always a traitor, somewhere. They just need to be weeded out."

Cato simply grins, which means that's all we're going to get out of them for tonight. In a city where knowledge was power, I didn't blame them for making sure they were taken care of. It was a dog-eat-dog world out there.

"I wonder how Julian's going to handle this?" Lola says, face thoughtful. "What would you do, if it were you?"

Drinking some of their wine, Cato nods. "One day it will be, and you'll have to give those orders."

"The Cartel currently occupies Meadowville, right?" I'm thinking out loud, not actually expecting an answer from either of them as I brush an egg wash over the pie, and pop it in the oven. "So, they're trying to expand more into the city in order to reach more clients and access our docks. Not forgetting our trading routes through Port Ellesmere and Silvercrest."

"Okay," Lola says slowly.

"So, I'd focus my energy on re-establishing my supply chain, I mean White Rabbit is double the quality and a decent price. Who's going to choose their toxic shit, mixed with God-knows what over that?" I set the timer on the oven, and take a swig of my wine, leaning back against the counter. "And while I'm at it, I'd get the Feds involved. Apply a little heat so The Cartel is preoccupied covering their asses and keeping their noses out of Family business. Then I'd send them a message. A big, bloody, gruesome one cutting them off at the knees."

Cato's mouth drops open as I smile wickedly at them. Turning to Lola, they look mildly disturbed as they shiver and pretend to bury their face in Lola's neck, hiding from me. "How can she say that so sincerely while baking a cherry pie like a little housewife?"

Lola just tosses her head back and laughs. "Because she's terrifying?"

Chapter Nine
Julian

"Hmm . . . What is it?" I ask groggily into the phone. It's a Sunday and Sundays are days designed specifically for a lay-in. With my hectic office schedule, and Family business keeping me occupied all hours of the day, I try to carve out a little bit of time every Sunday morning to stay in bed for just a little longer. I'd spent a fortune redecorating my bedroom last year, making it into a quiet space to unwind and yet I felt like I rarely got to spend time in my own bed.

A quick glance and my alarm clock tells me that it's 8:30 a.m. and I can barely keep my eyes open as the voice on the other end of the line tells me my presence is required downtown, in the Church Quarter. Sitting up, I swipe a hand over my face, trying to wake up and process the information coming at me.

An attack.

St Mary's.

Church Quarter.

Death.

So much pointless death.

When it finally sinks in, that an attack has been launched on one of our churches, I jump out of bed. Grabbing clothes from my walk-in wardrobe, I hastily throw them on, not bothering with a tie but taking time to brush my teeth and comb my hair. I was still a Family representative, and I still needed to present the right image even in the face of a crisis. A knock on my bedroom door tells me that Creed has arrived, and so taking the stairs two at a time, I head downstairs.

The Family has several churches that are frequented by members of the organization throughout Newtown but St Mary's was one of the largest. A design quirk of the city, or poor planning on the city's part, means that there's an area downtown not far from the docks where there are multiple churches built only streets apart, earning it the name 'The Church Quarter'. These churches aren't all ours, but it's where St Mary's sits and it's supposed to be neutral ground where people can pray and pay their respects but this...this is a violation of everything.

It's been eight days since I last saw Rosie Gambino. Eight long days and while I've been thinking of her, imagining her naked in my bed, remembering how she tastes, how she feels in my arms, she's been plotting. Planning how she's going to steal my kingdom out from underneath me, but this is a new low. Even for the Queen of Hearts.

We arrive at the church as the fire service extinguishes the last of the flames, the police cordoning off the immediate area as a small gathering of spectators watch. A news van pulls up, but the police keep them as far away from the scene as they can.

My heart aches at the blackened remains of the structure. Whatever remains of the shell crumbles and collapses in on itself under the weight of the water from the hose and a part of me shrivels up inside too.

There is no way survivors will be found.

There's nothing left.

One of the firemen speculates that this was a terrorist attack as it was definitely arson, but I know better. There's only one person in the world with this much hatred in their heart, and I've known it all along. I could have stopped this. I should have stopped this. These deaths were my fault, and once again I'm drowning in guilt.

I'm barely listening as the fire chief, who's one of us, explains that it appears the congregation were barricaded inside while gasoline was poured on the exits and set alight. Add in a few strategically placed flammables and the whole thing went up like a tinderbox. It would have been too fast to stop, especially on a sleepy Sunday morning when no one was expecting it. It wasn't just a mockery of the sanctity of the church and The Family, it was down-right cruel. Those people, my people, suffered for some petty games manipulated by a pretty blonde with a vendetta.

I thank him and his men for their work as he returns to shift through the rubble. I stand in silence, watching as they drag charred and unrecognizable bodies from the remains.

"Julian…" Elijah growls beside me. I can feel the anger radiating off him as we watch on the sidelines. My phone has constantly been ringing and I'd already called Daniel into the office to field calls. People were outraged. They were hurting and they wanted someone to be held accountable.

The Sunday school hadn't been spared either. Children were not part of this war and yet Rosalyn

Gambino had gone after them like the bloodthirsty bitch she is. I had been deluding myself when I thought I knew Rosalyn, she told me she was poisonous. She was the Queen of Hearts, a crown she wore proudly, so why hadn't I listened?

"Jules," Eli growls again, and I can feel the sob he's holding back as we see them bringing out bodies too small to be adults.

"I know."

He hisses, "She has to pay."

"I know!" I snap. Rosalyn has crossed a line and some things can't be taken back. I should know.

Antonio Bruno, my Consigliere, walks towards us. He's an older man in his early sixties, with greying hair and dark eyes. He's wearing a navy peacoat, a yellow scarf and a grey hat that he tips towards us as a sign of respect as he walks past and to his car. He was a friend of my father, and a staunch traditionalist but he was also my advisor, a role he took very seriously. My temples throb, warning of an impending headache. I knew I'd be hearing from him later regarding this situation and how he thought we should handle it.

Lawrence, one of my Captains, is close behind him. His dark inky black hair was slicked back and greying at the temples, his forehead heavily lined and pinched into a frown as he spotted Elijah and I. He had also been a friend of my father while he was still alive, and I wasn't under any illusions that Lawrence or Antonio particularly liked me or thought me capable, however they did have respect for hierarchy and convention, which worked in my favor. Most of the time.

"Julian, Creed," Lawrence intones as he glares at us. He has to look up at Elijah and I since he's barely five-foot-seven, something that seems to rankle him every time we talk like this. "I don't need to tell you this is unacceptable."

"Of course not, Lawrence." Eli bows his head, hoping his submission would defuse Lawrence's temper, but the shorter man balls his fists, features twisted with rage.

Jabbing a fat, pudgy finger into my shoulder, he gets close enough that I can smell stale cigarettes on his breath as he hisses into my face. "When I get my hands on that little bitch, I will make her pay for this. She will bleed. Her screams will be my new ringtone. I will fuck my wife to the sounds of her begging me for mercy. Do you understand?"

Without thinking, my hand darts out, and I grab the lapels of his coat. Lawrence was a sick son-of-a-bitch, who liked to torture people for fun. The things

I'd heard of him doing with hot irons and fire pokers made my skin crawl, and the only reason I kept him as a Captain was the loyalty he'd shown over the years to Belcastro and my father.

Yanking him to my chest, forcing him almost onto his tiptoes, I lean in and growl. "If you don't keep your hands off my...Rosalyn, there's going to be a problem. She is *my* issue, and it is *my* job as the head of this Family to punish her. Not yours."

Lawrence sputters, and if looks could kill I would be withering up in painful agony right about now. Sliding an arm between us, Eli puts some distance between me and Lawrence. He helps Lawrence smooth down his coat and we watch as the older man turns away in disgust.

"Oh, Lawrence," Eli calls, and we both give him hard stares. He sneers back at us, his bravery returning now that he was out of arm's reach. Tucking his jacket back so that his gun and hunting knife are exposed, Eli sucks his teeth, making a dismissive noise. "If you lay a finger on her without Julian's permission, I will remove all ten digits and shove them up your ass. Do you understand?"

Lawrence snorts, "Your little attack dog won't always be able to fight your battles Julian, you need to put this Family first. Are you strong enough for that?"

My cool facade back in place, I look down my nose at him as he climbs into his car and drives off. It seemed that if I wanted to keep a handle on the reins of my Family, I would need to capture a particularly stubborn filly and break her into a million pieces, so that she never rose again. I clench my fists, Eli and the other Family members weren't the only ones angry at this blatant and disgusting attack. An institution under the protection of The Family lies before me, nothing more than cinders and ash and I'd just defended the person responsible.

"What the fuck was that, man?" Eli whispers as we walk back towards where we'd parked. Glancing down at my phone, I wince, seeing twenty-nine missed calls and thirty-six messages. Damage control and reassurances were desperately needed before I made my way home tonight, it was going to be a long day.

"I...don't know." Fuck knows why I'd stepped in to lay some weird claim on her. I was planning on punishing her too, so what did it matter who did it? Except...except it did.

"Your Rosalyn?" Eli narrows his eyes, his anger still simmering away, like the embers glowering in the rear-view mirror as we drive to my office building.

"Shut up."

"Are you sure you can do what needs to be done?"
Elijah and I share a look.

"Family first, Eli. Always."

"A re you sure this is wise?" Elijah asks, as he adds a padlock to the basement door and fits a deadbolt high up, where I know Rosie will be unable to reach it. "Do you really want to keep her here?"

I nod, it wasn't like she didn't know where my offices were located. She sent me those damn hearts every year without fail. Rosalyn was my problem; and it was my responsibility to clean up the mess she'd made. I hadn't been able to get rid of her when I should have and now the deaths of twenty-four adults and eleven children were on my conscience. I could have prevented that. I could have stopped it from ever happening if I'd killed her years ago, or even when I first realized she was changing the rules on this little game of hers at the charity gala.

That's why I needed to be the one to punish her, to extract information about her little rebellion and what else they had planned. Then finally...I had to be the one to end it. There wasn't any other way this could go down. It had to be me. I'd played my role in turning her into a monster, and now I was going to reap what I'd sowed all those years ago.

I hadn't interrogated anyone personally for a while, purely because I didn't have time and one of the perks of being the head of an organization meant that I didn't have to do the wet-work anymore, unless I wanted to. Rosie was personal, and when her blood stained my hands, I'd finally get closure on my life and I'd be free.

"How're you going to find her?" Eli, using his keycard to access the elevator controls, guides us back upstairs to my office.

This wasn't a specific space we used for interrogations, those were dotted safely around the city, tucked away in various businesses and in some cases, homes. This was one we were making especially for her so I could keep a close eye on her away from the others. Away from Lawrence. I chuckle to myself bitterly; it was handy owning a building sometimes. I kept my legitimate businesses on the top floors, leaving the shadier dealings for the lower floors until you reached the basement, which would soon be a holding cell and interrogation chamber for Rosie. It was an inside joke, that the building was my dominion, offering up both heaven and hell, the floor you worked on reflecting your sins. It was only right that she was about to be chained up in the basement, like the devil she was.

"I may have some ideas..." I admit, a little sheepishly.

I had looked for her, especially in the beginning when I suspected she'd fled Newtown. It was before she earned her bloody moniker of Queen of Hearts, back when I'd still been a young man with foolish ideas of protecting her. Over the years, I'd kept an ear to the ground, paying for sightings and rumors out of my own pocket, but I was never able to verify them in time. Any trace of her vanished by the time I got there, and it was like chasing shadows. My father was furious each time I chased another dead end, the cold trails failures that reflected poorly on him. Every April and May, just before the murders and the arrival of the hearts, Belcastro, and then in turn myself, amped up the search, aiming to catch her before she made her kills. Hoping that she'd slip up and leave some evidence on the gifts or cards once they arrived, but she was meticulous.

Over the years I had eased back on the searching throughout the year, focusing on April and May. So while we still looked for her, it wasn't as hard as we should have been. The last couple of years, a few sightings began to form a pattern around her parents' graves and places special to them. I hadn't used it before, because I wasn't certain and I also held out some insane hope that Rosie would stop this rampage she was on when she saw what we were trying to do, the changes I was making.

"I fucking knew it!" Elijah slams his screwdriver down on my desk. "You are so pussy whipped over a pussy you haven't even seen. Typical Julian."

I raise a brow at him, his comment laughable. I've never been pussy whipped in my entire life because I only ever had casual relationships. Women weren't a permanent feature in my life and at thirty-two I had no plans to settle down just yet. There wasn't a woman in this town, who could understand the double life I led, except maybe one. And she was insane.

Reminded of the charred church, I can feel my mouth tighten into an angry line. "No. She's gone too far."

"She's been killing your men for years." He leans against the doorframe and gives me a pointed look. I was beginning to get fed up with Eli's judgmental expressions these days. I was aware that she was under my skin, that when it came to her, I wasn't as impartial or as rational as I should be. I didn't need him continually pointing it out.

I half shrug, aware that what I'm about to say is practically blasphemy. "My father's men. And her anger was understandable. It's also my fault for not keeping them safe."

There are a few moments of silence between us as his eyes widen and his mouth falls open.

Stepping towards me, he places a firm hand on my shoulder. "They're your men too, Jules. And she's not a toddler, she doesn't have to go around carving up men to make a point. I'm not even going to touch the last point, if you want to wallow in unnecessary guilt then that's your choice."

Shaking my head, I sit at my desk and bury my head in my hands. Memories of that night are burned into my brain like some sort of bad horror film. Even the memories of her looking beautiful and almost fae-like in the gardens don't take away all the gore. "You weren't there, Eli. Her whole house was drowning in blood. It was . . . I've never seen anything like it."

I can hear his soft footfalls as he comes closer and pats my back. "That wasn't you, Julian. You need to stop taking responsibility for everyone and every-thing. You aren't Felix and you aren't Frank."

I know that I'm not my father, but I can't let the things he did go. I can't forget the pain he caused, just the same as I can't forget what Rosalyn has done.

There are consequences to our actions, and sometimes lessons need to be taught to understand that. If they had to be enlightened through pain and bloodshed, even though I'd done my best to avoid it, then so be it.

"I have to make things right," I say, my voice resolute.

Eli nods slowly. "If you hurt a dog, and years later it became crazy and started attacking people—innocent people—what would you do?"

"Put it down."

The answer is so clear cut when it's framed like that—when it's an us versus them situation, when it's loyal supporters and rebels or traditionalists versus anarchists, but when it's just Jay and Rosie, there are only shades of grey.

He narrows his eyes at me. "Remember that. You're offering her kindness by putting her out of her misery."

"Yes," I whisper, my chest tight. But who's going to put me out of mine?

Chapter Ten

Rosie

I don't know where I am.

I can't see anything.

My hands are tied.

Don't panic Rosie, deep breaths and think. *This is what you're good at*, I tell myself as I calm my racing heartbeat and control my breathing. This is hardly the first time I'd found myself in a situation like this, and I was always prepared, like the good little girl scout I never was.

I'd been visiting my parents' graves, laying white roses on their headstones in the wake of the church fire. That had been their church, St Mary's, the one they had gotten married in all those years ago. It was where I was baptized and where we went every Sunday for service. I remember sitting in the hard, cold pews as a teenager, hating the way the prayer cushion itched beneath my knees and the priest spoke like in a dull monotone. I remember my father looking so serious in his suit, but whenever he would catch my eye, he'd pull a funny face, making me laugh until my mother, in her Sunday best, would give us both a glare and silence us both. It was where the Christmas carol service and mass was held each year, where we'd drink mulled wine, watch a nativity retelling from the Sunday school children and light candles in prayer, thankful for the things we had in our lives.

It was where their funerals had been held, in secret of course since Belcastro and Felix had tried to deny me that, even though churches were supposed to be neutral territory. When I'd heard that my tio Matteo had stolen their bodies, I'd risked everything to return to Newtown for the funeral, scattering their ashes in the family plot with Lola and Matteo as the only witnesses. That church was tied up in so many memories of my parents, and now it was gone, just like they were. Everything that tied me to them had been ripped away and yet I was the bad guy.

When I find out who had disobeyed my orders and used me in their campaign against Julian, I am going to skin them alive and make a coat out of their flesh. I had specifically instructed them not to get innocent bystanders and Family members involved. There were kids inside the building. Children who'd done nothing. I brought thirty-five roses with me, one for each life lost and I couldn't stop the tears that came as I laid them down. Death was part of Family life, but this was wrong. This has crossed a line and someone has to pay for that.

I'd sat on the grass in silence, praying for the lives lost, for those left behind to deal with the pain, surrounded by white roses that were already fading, discoloring slowly as they decayed. I'd heard soft footsteps, as someone approached from behind but I'd just assumed it was Cassie, one of my Captains, who'd accompanied me here this morning as she'd come to lay flowers on her daughter's grave. That assumption had cost me, as I'd been knocked out cold.

And that's how I'd woken up here, tied to a chair with rope and a pretty complicated knot by the feel of it. Someone was worried I'd be able to escape, clearly. Sometimes the rumors and legends of my bloodthirsty nature were a help, others, like this, they were a hindrance.

Footsteps above me and the faint smell of damp and stale air makes me think I'm below street level, a basement or a cellar maybe? I can't hear any running water but I can hear the hum of traffic. Am I downtown? From what I can tell, I still have my clothes on and while my stiletto blade, handgun and my throwing knives have been removed, my ring hasn't. I carefully twist the band around and using a virtually invisible button disguised as a rose filigree, a tiny blade pops out from behind the large black oval stone. It's a thin short razor blade, but it's enough to start cutting the rope. I shake my head a little, and my hair stays in place, which means my hairpins are still in and they're sharpened, ready for situations like this.

I haven't spent ten years in hiding and on the run to learn nothing and poisonous hairpins were only the tip of the iceberg. The streets of East Point served to teach me the things my father didn't, and I had learned a lot about survival there. You have to get inventive sometimes in order to stay alive, you can't be afraid to get your hands bloody. It wasn't like Newtown, where there was a clear hierarchy, where one group dominated. Fighting to survive in East Point made Newtown look like a picnic in the park.

Hearing voices getting closer, I freeze. I can't risk them finding my ring. There's something familiar about the huskiness I can hear as it nears...it sounds like...

"Jay!" I exclaim with a grin, as a man I recognize as the Left Hand of The Family pulls the bag off my head. He's cute, his dark hair tied up in a messy bun, a scar cutting through his left eyebrow just above intense dark eyes but his face is too serious for my liking. He's a mountain of a man, but I'd know that from my surveillance. At almost six foot five, he stood a few inches taller than Julian but he was wider, more muscular and that made sense since he was supposedly Julian's protection as well as his errand boy.

My gaze shifts, to where Julian stands in a designer navy suit, green eyes narrowed, the color dimmed by the basement lighting. He's oddly serious today too, staying back with his arms crossed, his mouth pulled into a tight line as he glares down at me.

"You could have just called if you missed me," I tease with a smile and a flutter of my lashes knowing full well that he doesn't have my number but his face remains cold. "No need to go to extremes."

In the periphery I clock only one exit located just behind Julian. It's electronically locked, which means one of them has to be holding a keycard. There are pipes and fuse boxes down here, but the chair I'm sitting on is the only piece of furniture. The lighting is dull and yellow. I think I'm in his building's basement, which is interesting. Why bring me here and not to one of the Family interrogations rooms? What was he planning?

"Rosalyn, stop," he commands, forcing my attention back to him. "You've gone too far this time."

Tilting my head, I frown. "I'm sorry sweetie, I don't understand . . ."

Crack!

Julian's Left Hand man just used his right hand on my cheek, slapping me while Julian glances away, avoiding my gaze like a coward. My face stings, and heat blossoms across my skin. Running my tongue over the inside of my mouth, I can't taste blood, so he hasn't done any actual damage.

I wiggle my jaw, opening my mouth before I turn my head back to face them. "Creed, isn't it? Trust me when I say, you will regret that. I promise you."

"I don't give a damn about your empty threats, you piece of shit," he hisses as he grabs a handful of my hair, yanking my head back roughly. It jolts my body enough to distract them from the fact I'm slowly getting through the rope.

"Have we met before? No?" I grin obnoxiously, provoking him. "Then be a dear, and zip it. I have a killer headache and just seeing your face is making me feel queasy."

With a roll of my eyes, I sigh dramatically. That earns me another backhand, this time he cuts my lip. I can taste bitter copper and that's fine, it just fuels my resolve. This isn't my first kidnapping situation. And it's certainly not my first interrogation. I've endured worse and survived.

Julian remains silent, but at least he's looking at me now, his emerald eyes locked with mine as he stands in the shadows. He's hiding from me, from what's being done to me and that's why my Captains think he's too weak to lead them. You can't be in charge of an organization like The Family, where violence is part of our legacy, where people get hurt and people die, and be afraid of inflicting a little pain. I suck on my split lip and moan, the noise low and sultry. Julian's cheek twitches and I smirk.

"Beautiful but crazy, isn't that what you said Jules?" Creed smirks as he grabs my chin sharply. "Why did you lie? She's a hideous person, inside and out."

"Awh, you called me beautiful?"

That earns me another slap.

This one is harder and for a moment my eyes struggle to focus, my brain rattled against my skull but I don't let on. Just a little more, I just need to keep going until . . .

"Oh, you have no idea, baby," I laugh as I feel warm liquid trickle down my chin and my ropes loosen. I think both my nose and my lip are bleeding freely now, but I can't say for sure until I can separate the pain. My words are said to Creed, but it's still Julian I'm watching. He's furious, and even though he looks calm and disinterested as he lurks by the door, I can see the way his eyes flash. The rage that surrounds him is barely noticeable, if you didn't know him, if you didn't understand how he worked. But I knew him better than anyone, I'd spent years learning how he thought.

This is about the church. It has to be.

He really thought I was responsible and he wasn't even going to give me a chance to explain. Fucking coward. He was going to bow to pressure from his Captains and the elders without looking at the facts first. What did I have to gain from burning down a church? From killing children?

The others were right, he was weak.

"Are you getting a kick out of this?" Creed leans in and bellows in my face, spittle hitting my cheek. "You're more fucked up than I thought."

"Wouldn't you like to know," I whisper before licking his face with a satisfied groan.

It startles him and he jumps back, cursing as he

tries to wipe away the stripe of my blood and spit that marks him. With him distracted, I use the time I've just bought myself to jump into action, springing up and knocking his feet out from under him. He lands on his back with a satisfying thud and a huge exhale of air, and I think I hear the distinct crack of a rib or two on the cold concrete.

Before he can recover, I'm crouched over him, pinning both his arms to the cold concrete floor with my knees, my razor ring blade pressed against the artery in his neck, my free hand firmly on his throat. Just a little bit of pressure from me, and Elijah Creed would become nothing more than a myth in Newtown's Family history as another one of my victims. When I carved him open, I would make sure he felt every single cut. Every incision. I might actually eat his heart, just to spite him for the way my face hurts.

"They don't call me a killer Queen for nothing, baby," I hiss, invading his personal space like he'd done to me. "And I did warn you."

The man beneath me looks to his king and frowns as Julian says nothing. Jay doesn't want to do anything rash; he doesn't want to risk me killing one of his best men and so he watches, waits for my cue. It's admirable, but a weakness I fully intend to exploit. After all, this is the game we've been playing for years.

"It looks like Jay isn't going to help you, are you surprised?" I ask in a sad voice, as I lean in close, grinning as blood drips from my mouth and nose onto his skin. Thick, ruby splotches landing with fat plopping noises as he flinches with every drop. "Don't worry sweetie, Rosie will take care of you."

I kiss the tip of his nose and chuckle as he growls at me. Taking my hand from his throat I quickly reach up and grab the hairpin with a flower on the end. Creed tries to move, to take back control, but I dig the blade into his skin just enough to bite and he goes still. Smart man. Taking the pin, I stab it into his neck, and before he even registers what I've done his eyes are rolling back into his head and he's unconscious.

"Was that necessary?" Julian finally says as I stand and brush the dust off my dress.

"Was this?" I ask, waving my hand around the dank cellar before pointing to my fat, bleeding lip and bloody face. Pressing my fingers into my skin gently, I work out that my nose isn't broken, just sore and the gash in my lip is my only real injury. I scoff as I look down at Elijah Creed, the man couldn't even hurt me enough to leave a scar. This was Julian's protection?

"Yes. You crossed a line." His words are tight, said

through gritted teeth as he reaches into his pocket and pulls out a handkerchief. He offers it to me and I accept, ignoring the way my skin tingles where our fingers brush.

Mopping up the blood from my face and following the trail of crimson that had managed to fall down into my cleavage, I raised a brow. "You mean the church?"

"Of course, I mean the church." He narrows his eyes at me suspiciously. "Why, what else have you done?"

I place my hands on my hips and laugh. "So many, many things. But this one wasn't me."

Chapter Eleven
Julian

I don't believe her.

She's a liar.

A liar who's crossed the line. I knew she'd try to escape, that's why I held back, I wanted to see how far she'd go. Clearly, poison is her party trick since this is the second time she'd resorted to it, and I make a mental note to get Elijah to strip her completely naked next time. We'd removed her weapons and her heels, but obviously the woman couldn't even be trusted with a hair ornament. I silence the small voice in the back of my head that's impressed with her little show, not many men could incapacitate Creed, let alone a woman who was barely five foot six. Her father would be proud of the fighter he'd created.

Well, maybe not given how easy it was to capture her at her parents' graveside. I'd sent Eli and two of his most trusted men to where her family home used to sit on the outskirts of Newtown on the edge of the suburbs. It was all gone now, destroyed after that night, except for the family cemetery. My father had been furious when he found out that the priest at St Mary's had delivered a service for Amara and Vincent Gambino. Even more livid when their bodies had vanished right under his nose. I remember that night vividly, because it had been the night he'd broken my cheek bone.

He had nursed his sixth glass of whiskey, staring into the fireplace as he listened to Riccardo Baroni, another Captain, explaining that Amara and Vincent's bodies were missing from the morgue. There were no witnesses and only grainy CCTV footage from a camera belonging to a store opposite the building. It showed nothing. My father always was a sore loser, and the fact that an eighteen-year-old girl had somehow managed to evade The Family and take back something he had confiscated, that rankled. He'd pulled out his mother of pearl Damascus switchblade and cut Riccardo's pinky finger clean off without even blinking. Riccardo had let him; the man had barely cried out as the useless digit landed on the rug with a soft thud. That was the power of Felix Asaro, he made grown men quake in their boots, afraid of worse punishments than just losing a finger. Once Riccardo had been dismissed, that was when he really lost it. He'd smashed the bottle of whiskey against the wall, a shard cutting my cheek as glass and amber liquid flew everywhere in an explosion of rage. I'd flinched, making a surprised noise and that's when his dark gaze had zeroed in on me. He made me the outlet for his rage, fists relentless as he cursed Rosalyn Gambino over and over again. And I bit my cheeks, clenched my fists, swallowed back the pain and endured it, because it was the least I could do. I deserved it for betraying her.

They never discovered who'd taken the bodies, but I suspected she had them cremated afterwards, since it was harder to steal back ashes and dust. And my father would have tried to steal their corpses back, he was that twisted in his anger and spite. He was determined that Rosie should be left with nothing. He almost succeeded too.

She stands before me, angry and defiant, and it burns. Her hair is mussed, one pin still barely holding her curls back as it starts to unfurl. Bloody face, blue eyes shining, she drives me wild. The way she'd taunted Eli, laughing and flirting as he'd hit her. She was fucked up. Broken beyond repair, and Eli's words came back to haunt me. Put her out of her misery.

Striding toward her, I hiss but she doesn't even blink. Stormy blue eyes watch me, pupils wide and it's like she's a snake, poised and waiting for the right moment to strike. She doesn't flinch as I grab her throat and squeeze. I could crush her windpipe, force her to her knees, I could end this right now. The tension between us throbs, aching like a headache that refuses to die. Her lips part as she seems to relax into my grip. I want to snap her pretty little neck almost as much as I want to fuck her, what kind of monster does that make me?

I feel every sensation as she tries to swallow, her skin warm against mine as she tries to suck in air but still, she says nothing. She doesn't lash out at me, nor does she try to move away. Her hands twitch a little by her sides as she clutches my handkerchief but other than that, she stays still. I squeeze, tightening my grip. Rosalyn Gambino stands, perfectly still like a good little girl, while I choke her and that's how I know something doesn't add up. I step back and cross my arms once again. Why is she looking at me like that?

"Are we done already? I was rather enjoying that."

Her breathing is uneven and I'm not sure it's from my attempt to frighten her, especially not given the wolfish grin she's giving me.

"Have you no respect?" I spit.

She mimics my pose and I try to ignore the way it makes her tits even more noticeable, even with the blood covering her like a damn Rorschach test. What would my results reveal? That I was beyond help? That this woman had burrowed her way under my skin and I was dying as I tried to claw her out again? I flick my eyes back to her face, ignoring her tits and her clothes. Who the hell visits their parents' final resting place in a low cut, navy polka dot tea dress with red heels? Why was life just one giant fashion show for her? She looked like some pin-up model, not a mafia princess in hiding. It was like she was waiting for me to find her. Taunting me.

Snorting, she runs a bloody hand through her hair, refastening it with her remaining pin. "For those who deserve it. And you don't. Not if you think I had anything to do with this."

"Who the fuck else would do this? Who else wants to hurt me that badly?" I practically scream and I try to ignore the flash of hurt I read on her face. She has no right to be hurt. How dare she? She brought this on herself.

Her lips twist into a snarl as she shouts back, "I don't kill children, you should know better than that."

"Do I?" I scoff, running a hand through my hair as I begin pacing around the cellar. Eli is still unconscious and being trapped in here with Rosie is dangerous, I can smell her, that sweet cherry cinnamon scent tinged with blood and sweat. Permeating everything. Invading everything. All my senses were consumed by her. There was no way I could let her go. Not now, not ever. If I did, I'd always be looking over my shoulder and any more deaths by her hands would be on my conscience. I could see it now, the bodies continuing to pile high, until I was buried beneath them, gasping for air. There was no escaping Rosalyn Gambino.

"You send me the hearts of men every year on your birthday, but killing children is too much?" I remind her cruelly, my words cutting and she has the gall to slap me.

Grabbing her wrist, I turn her and pin her against my chest, trapping her in the vice of my arms. It's to protect my face from another attack, but damn if it doesn't provoke the pervert inside me. I wonder if she'd be just as pliant on her knees, if the view would be just as sinful. From here I can see straight down her bloody slicked cleavage as her body pressed against mine, and I inhale that dark cherry scent wafting up from her skin. She must bathe in pie filling, the way it lingers around her.

I can feel her anger subside, as she melts into my touch, whispering, "Those men deserved it. They were traitors, they betrayed my family and they left me orphaned. I lost everything."

I sigh, loosening my grip. "That wasn't your call. The head of the Family . . ."

"Was corrupt. Twisted by power." She tries to push against me, but I keep a hold on her and we stand, wrapped up in one another. I've let her go too many times; today was the last time she'd get away. When she realizes that I'm not budging she goes still and that sends a wave of apprehension through me, making me more nervous. A calm, clear-headed Rosie is a dangerous one.

Frank Belcastro had been my mentor, and a close friend of my father's but that didn't mean I was incapable of recognizing his flaws. He was greedy, desperate for power and in his later years, he'd become gluttonous with it. It had driven him to the brink of insanity, as he'd been convinced that everyone was out to steal from him, believing we were all plotting his downfall. He'd died after a short battle with cancer, it had been brutal and almost soul destroying to watch as he'd gone from being a powerful, vindictive man to a shell, husked out and withering from the inside. I'd sat by his bedside, kept him informed of all Family business and proved my worth as one of his Captains. I did as was expected of me, as my father demanded and that was why no one was surprised when Frank nominated me as his successor. I knew he was twisted by his own greed. I knew he was paranoid. I also knew that Vincent Gambino wasn't as innocent as Rosie seemed to think. The man was like a god to her, and I wasn't going to be the one to unearth all of his sins. Not only because she wouldn't believe me, but because his memory had suffered enough.

Her voice doesn't falter as she straightens her shoulders, still trapped. "They were grown men who made grown-up choices and had to pay for the decisions they made."

She isn't wrong. Actions come with repercussions, especially in organized crime. Did she not see the irony in the situation? Her avenging angel routine, a figurehead fighting for justice and killing those she perceived as having wronged her, those were also grown-up choices and there were only ever two possible outcomes. Her death...or mine.

"Then who would do this?" I don't know why I should believe her, but I do. Even though she's a killer, a liar, a vixen determined to end me and yet...I hear the honesty in her words. She has a point; she's never shied away from the crimes she's committed. In fact, she sent cards privately claiming her little trophies and publicly she may as well write her name on them in red lipstick. The media loved the Queen of Hearts, always speculating on who the angry, twisted woman might be killing of Newtown's men. Anyone within The Family recognized the connections between the deaths, and that's why it was common knowledge who the Queen was amongst our circles. She was the boogeyman we told our children about to keep them in line. That's why it made no sense for her to deny this crime, these deaths would be nothing to her and yet she was vehement in her innocence.

I can practically hear her rolling her eyes as she says, "Someone who wants both of us gone."

"What have I got to do with any of this? Your little rebellion is the one being framed." I frown, I haven't got any issues with my handle on the Family other than her. She was the one undermining me at every turn, causing people to think I was weak. Belcastro had selected me as his successor and no one else besides Rosie ever dared to challenge my authority to my face.

Her voice is quiet again. "You're weak Jay, always

were." It's like she's trying to let me down softly. "And this act of cruelty is designed to expose that and blame me. We're both being tried in this Family courtroom."

She has a point. I know that while I have a hold on the reins, there are whispers that I'm not willing to get my hands dirty enough. People in the shadows are quick to criticize the choices I make and the way I like to explore every option before resorting to violence. Greed, desire and shame are all powerful motivators, I'd learned that quickly over the years and that's why I put pressure on those points before I drew my gun. Even though the Family elders are respectful in public, I know many of them believe that I have turned my back on the old ways. I mean, that's how Rosie was able to garner support behind my back. There was something about her ruthless, bloodthirsty nature that gained respect from the old school members. They didn't seem to understand that the days of suave, charming, slick mafioso's were gone. Today technology and money motivated the world, and we needed to work smarter on this new playing field.

"So, what now?"

It hasn't escaped my attention that Rosie has relaxed into my hold, and for some reason we've begun to gently sway as if we were lovers embracing and not enemies destined to kill one another.

She sighs, almost melting into me. "I don't know, but I need to clear my name. Someone is gunning for us and I refuse to have infanticide added to my list of crimes. I won't have that done in my name."

If someone wants to bring us both down, if they think they can turn us against each other then we need to find a way to work together. There was already too much uncertainty in the air in Newtown. With The Cartel trying to interfere with White Rabbit distribution and Lev Volkov disappearing from the public eye, making me nervous about our weapons suppliers, the last thing I needed was to be called incompetent for failing to deal with the terror that is the Queen of Hearts. It was like everything was balancing precariously on my shoulders as I tried to walk a tightrope, only one good gust of wind from dropping it all.

"I might have a suggestion but he's not going to like it," I murmur as Elijah groaned from the floor behind us as he took his involuntary nap.

Chapter Twelve

Rosie

I walk around the plush mini mansion that Julian owns, nestled away in the suburbs. We'd driven up a long gravel driveway to a large grey stone building with a smaller separate building beside it, likely a garage. There had been staff tending to the gardens, cutting the trees and mowing the grass as we passed but he'd quickly dismissed the housekeeping staff for the remainder of the day once we'd entered the large double front doors.

The entryway was large and airy, featuring a grand staircase with twisted metal balusters and real wood flooring. We move through into a lounge area, where I run my hands over everything, reminding myself that this life should have been mine.

Photos of him and Creed, various awards he's gained for his charity work in Newtown and newspaper articles are framed and on display. There's even a picture of his parents in a silver burnished frame. I wordlessly knock it face down on the sideboard as we pass, feeling satisfied when I hear the glass crack. Julian glares at me, but says nothing of my pettiness.

Three large leather sofa's form a U shape around a walnut coffee table, facing the large ornate fireplace and I smile, imagining chilly winter evenings spent curled up watching the fire crackle. The wall opposite is completely covered with books, the large floor to ceiling shelves stacked with law texts, classic literature, and well-worn paperbacks. Jealousy pangs in my chest and I swallow uncomfortably. I haven't been able to buy and keep books for a long time, since I had nowhere to store them and I jumped around between my followers and Lola. Her tiny apartment barely had space for her small crappy TV, let alone a bookcase. The whole house smells like him, like books and coffee.

We finally settled in his home office, a room filled with dark woods and more books.

He sits at his desk, a large bespoke piece with

intricately carved legs and I can tell how much he cherishes it, the wood gleaming and perfectly polished.

"If you want me to stay here, I have conditions."

"I don't want you here Rosie." He looks up at me over the edge of the papers he's holding. His green eyes flash, and not for the first time do I wonder how he ended up with eyes like that and his tarnished gold hair, when both his parents had been dark haired and dark eyed. True Italian genetics shone through in them, and while Julian had Felix's features, his strong nose, clean cut jawline, there was none of Lina in her son. Interesting.

"Don't lie." I fall back onto the couch near another ornate fireplace with carved dragons and laugh. "Someone wants to bring us down; we don't have time for lies."

Julian wants me, it's the one thing I'm certain of right now and I'd be the one lying if I said I wasn't thinking about him naked. Our little dinner, where I'd left him behind, had only served to show me just how explosive it could be between us. The hate we harbored for one another, was so close to love it was painful. The life we could have had together taunted us at every turn, and every explosive touch, every lingering gaze was just a reminder that he had betrayed me and now everything was ruined.

I push off my heels, making a show of rubbing my feet and calves, digging my thumbs in with small groans, pretending that I can't feel his eyes on me. The sharp intake of breath that I almost miss as I begin rolling down my snagged and ripped stockings, makes something in my chest flutter and I have to bite down on my bottom lip to stop myself from making a flippant comment.

I grin as I hear him swallow. "Fine, let's hear your terms."

Jay had already made it very clear that no one was to know I was here, in fact he'd started putting out rumors that I was dead. The Queen of Hearts vanquished by the great Julian Asaro, the very capable and handsome head of The Family, as retribution for the desecration of St Mary's. Even though I was innocent. His little ploy would supposedly help us flush out whoever wanted both of us so tied up in one another, we overlooked them. He also cut off my communication with my people by confiscating my possessions, and I was forbidden from leaving the grounds. No one, not even Lola and Cato knew that I was still alive, lounging on a sofa that cost more than my entire wardrobe of thrifted and hand-me-down clothes.

Not that I minded in the short term, Julian had a huge pool with beautiful gardens and a kitchen I wanted to live in. I haven't had a permanent home since mine was destroyed, literally since Belcastro had it burned to the ground and I had to move to keep from being found. I couldn't risk it. I had been living on the streets, squatting with Lola, sofa surfing, bed-hopping and imposing on my supporters over the last ten years. Having one place to hide away for a while sounded like bliss, it was definitely more like a holiday than a prison sentence. One I intended to make the most of.

I sigh dramatically, holding up my ruined stockings. Elijah Creed owes me a new pair and I'll make sure I get them before I leave, even if I have to strangle him with the old pair first to get them.

Tossing the destroyed hosiery aside, I sit back and tap my fingers against my lips. "I want your room."

He thinks I'm being difficult; I can see it in the way his lips pull into a tight line and I resist the urge to climb across his desk and grab his chin before forcing his lips apart with my tongue. "Why? There are three other guest rooms here. Pick one of them."

Unfastening the front buttons on my bloody, dirty

dress, I allow it to pop open and reveal my lace bra. I send up a silent thank you to all the deities that I'd decided to wear nice, matching underwear today. "No. I want yours."

"Anything else?" He looks away, and I can't stop the butterflies in my stomach. I didn't intend to seduce him...I just wanted to play with him a little. I couldn't turn down the opportunity to make him squirm as I got what I wanted.

"A fully stocked kitchen and my weapons back." Standing, I push the dress down over my shoulders and let it fall. When it gets stuck at my waist, I shimmy it the rest of the way down. Curse my mother and her Welsh heritage for giving me hips that men literally die for.

"Yes, to the first, no way in hell to the second." Julian fixes me with a stare as he tries to avoid glancing at my bare skin. "I don't want you to kill me in my sleep."

"Fine." Smiling, I lay down on his couch, hand over my head like some sort of artist's model as I lounge virtually naked on his furniture. I never expected him to agree to give me my blade and my gun back, but it was worth asking. Besides, I was good with my hands and you'd be surprised how many things around the home could be weaponized. My uncle Alessio had taught me how to use what I had to hand, so I wouldn't always be reliant on specific toxins or chemicals. The results were usually crude, but they came in handy.

When I'd killed Frankie Rossi, I'd had to pose as a personal chef for almost a month. He didn't trust me, and would have me patted down at the beginning and end of every shift. His paranoia meant he'd sent his family away, only keeping a skeleton crew as staff. I was only allowed to use the produce he supplied, and I was watched closely by the man he'd hired as security.

Well...let's just say my oral skills make me very trustworthy with big burly bodyguards and house-hold bleach should never be mixed with vinegar. Especially not if your bodyguard is incapacitated in a broom closet and your chef wants to carve out your heart. Rigging his dining room to release chlorine gas through his meal was one of the easiest things I'd ever done since he'd sent all the staff except me and the bodyguard home. I lingered outside once I'd served him, listening as he'd sputtered and coughed. I'd had to bite down on the back of my knuckles to keep from laughing as he got to his feet and stumbled around. The second I heard Frankie's body hit the floor, I'd opened the windows and dragged him into the kitchen where I tied him to a chair. I apparently have a fetish for tying men to chairs. I wonder what that says about me?

He'd been a portly man once, a giant to my eighteen-year self, but the man before me was old and thin. His cheeks were hollowed and his skin waxy as he came around, looking at me with terrified eyes. He had known, just like the others that his days were numbered. He screamed louder than any of the rest had when I began cutting into him. Cracking his chest was nowhere near as satisfying as it should have been and when I'd carefully packaged up his shriveled little heart, I briefly wondered if it was because I still had his sons on my list.

"Is that all?" Julian shuffles some papers around on his desk, bringing me out of my memories, before loosening his tie. He looks tired and I resist the urge to get up and massage his shoulders. He's not my lover, he's not even my partner . . . he's just Julian. Jay. The boy with the floppy gold hair, who stole my first kiss, who betrayed my family and has spent the last ten years playing games with me like it was some sort of secret code between us. We defied common sense. We can't be explained by rationality because we're both monsters who lurk in the shadows and we're intertwined in a way that transcends common sense.

"For now..." I say as I twirl my hair in my fingers lazily. He should have killed me already. I should have destroyed him. But here we are. "Where is Creed?"

Elijah Creed was a strange man. He'd been by Julian's side since they were young despite their fathers often being opposed to one another, according to my sources. Augustine Creed had been a fighter, a man dragged up on streets who fought tooth and nail for everything he had and when Belcastro made him a Captain, and put him in charge of running The Gryphon, the underground boxing ring, he'd been happy with his lot in life. He was hard on his son, forcing him to fight and like many other parents within The Family, using his fists to discipline his child. Felix Asaro had that in common with him at least. Felix had been hungry for power, it was why he'd practically licked Belcastro's asshole, in hopes of progressing his family and he didn't care who he had to fuck, kill or maim to work his way up the greasy pole. So how did the two of them ever become friends? What drew them together?

"He's doing a little digging for me into who else could have done this. We've been having...some issues."

It had to be someone who would gain from us taking each other out, someone who knew that the church was a line that couldn't be crossed for either side. I think back to the meeting and unease settles in my stomach. There were many discontented voices there that night, and betrayal was always lingering. Trust was a fragile thing, like a butterfly. Hold on to it too hard, rely on it too much and you'd crush it in the palm of your hands. What good is a butterfly with broken wings?

Esme and Valentina would be at the top of my list logically, since Esme had one of the biggest grudges to settle and Valentina was a nasty old bitch. Esme wasn't cold hearted enough; I don't think she has it in her to hurt innocents. Especially not children. Valentina, well, she was the wicked witch who lived in the woods in someone's story.

"Hmmmm, yes. Cartel. White Rabbit. Russians. Want me to take those issues off your hands, Jay?" I make a pouting face, teasing him as I ignore his eye roll and muttering.

He grumbles, placing the papers flat on his desk. "Of course you know everything."

Whoever planned would have to either be a part of The Family, or they would have had insider knowledge. There weren't many things that would force Jay to lash out at me in anger. I had killed so many men and women over the years hunting down those who'd played their roles in my parents' betrayal, and yet, they knew this was one of them.

This little stunt was forcing him into a corner. Either he dealt with me brutally, thus taking me out of the equation and out of the running for the crown in our little game of power or he stayed silent and was shown to be weak. That hesitation from him would only serve to show how unfit he was to oversee The Family, meaning the little mastermind behind this could come in and steal control legitimately.

"What did you say about me? He wants me dead." Creed didn't scare me, in fact I had a strange respect for him. I had heard the rumors surrounding Augustine Creed and his discipline for both his child and his wife, everyone had. Hell, when I knocked Creed on his ass, I felt the scars carved into his skin, almost buried beneath the tattoos. Anyone who can survive that, and still pledge loyalty to this Family was crazy, and I liked crazy.

Sounding tired Julian groans, "I said I was going to take care of it."

I can't stop chuckling, as I wiggle my toenails, the red paint dancing. "So, he thinks you're putting me out to pasture right now, instead of sprawling on your couch?"

Boy, was that man in for a surprise, especially

when he found me here, in Julian's home, making myself comfortable. And I intended to make myself *very* comfortable. What did it say about our little game that the King of the castle hadn't even told his best and only friend about his plan? This little act of secrecy was yet another crack I intended to exploit at a later date.

"Something like that..." His phone rings, he checks the name, and given the way he winces, I assume it's the man himself. He swipes, refusing the call and then places his phone screen down.

"And when this is over?" I don't want to ask, but I have to. The fact that I was here, still gathering tidbits to use against him like it was second nature to me despite our momentary truce makes me spit out the words.

We're still enemies, we still have a complicated past and neither of us can wash that away. Our hands are stained with it, the pain and bloodshed, mine more than his. I cannot just step back while he continues living the life that should have been mine. Using the powers that should have been given to me.

"We'll deal with it then."

"Where will you be sleeping tonight?" I stand with a stretch, breaking the tension that had crept back into our conversation.

"In the guest room next to yours, I suppose. Try not to murder me in the middle of the night. I rather like breathing." The way Julian watches my body move almost makes me want to do a whole yoga session in front of him, but I think that may be a little extreme. Even for me.

"Well, night," I mumble before quietly leaving the room, making sure my hips sway just a little more as I go, my cream thong and bra doing the job they should as I feel his gaze on me again. Even if a little blood has ruined them by soaking through my dress.

It isn't hard to find Julian's bedroom; it's got his personality stamped all over it. Dark bottle green walls, crisp white sheets, dark woods and more stacks of books and papers everywhere, it's all very masculine and him.

The first thing I do is strip off my underwear, shower and crawl between the soft sheets. I'm engulfed by the scent of him and as I bury myself in the covers, I wish things were different, but it's only for a fleeting moment because it stings and I don't want to think about what comes after. I lay awake thinking about Jay, how I felt like I knew him almost as well as I knew myself, which should be impossible given how little time we've actually spent together.

It's around midnight when I hear soft footfalls

outside the door, and the guest room door opening and closing. Grinning to myself, I push the covers down, cupping my breasts. Moaning louder than I normally would, I spread my legs, relishing how the expensive sheets feel against my clean skin. My hands explore the soft lines of my body, trailing down my sternum, between my breasts, up over the hard nubs, back down along my ribs. Lower and lower, in no rush, enjoying the sensations it sends through me.

I slide two fingers through the slickness gathering between my legs, pinching my nipple hard with my other hand. Another groan leaves me. It's him. It's knowing he's next door, that he can hear me. It's being surrounded by the scent of him, tangling myself up in his sheets as I play with myself. I slow down, getting too close, too quick.

My pussy throbs, swollen and sensitive as I imagine him sitting between my legs, encouraging me, telling me what a good girl I am. The fantasy has me almost whimpering. Would he fuck me hard and fast, or would he drag it out painfully? Teasing me until my cunt was dripping and I was desperate for him? Would he wrap my hand around his fist and bite down on my neck as he ploughed into me? Maybe he would worship every inch of my skin with those large hands of his, his mouth and tongue desperate to taste me, to mark me, to claim me.

"Fuck. Fuck. *Fuckkkkk.*" I call out loudly as I come, clenching the sheets with one hand and covering my pussy with the other, feeling it clench and pulse around an imaginary cock.

Leaning back into the sheets, I hear muffled noise coming from the room next door. Followed by the shower running. There weren't many things I was certain of, but this was one of them: Julian Asaro's cock would be inside me before the end of the week.

Chapter Thirteen
Julian

I t's been hell.

Absolute hell as Rosie has walked around my house wearing next to nothing. I'd sent my staff out for some clothes, all designer, all according to her tastes but she is refusing to wear them saying that she should feel comfortable while she's here.

I've been working from home to keep an eye on her, one of the perks of being the boss of my own firm and the head of a crime organization, but she's been nothing but a distraction. One the first day, I'd walked into her 'greeting the sun' wearing nothing but one of my workout vests and a pair of my boxers stretched across her ass as she'd moved from one pose to another. When she noticed me and moved into a more upright position, all I could think about was how I could see her nipples poking through the thin fabric of my vest. None of which was helped by the fact that I'd listened to her come the night before in my fucking bed. Or that I'd come, only moments after before making myself take a cold shower.

The second day, after another repeat of her nightly orgasm and my new cold shower routine, she decided to swim all day. This time she accepted one of the swimsuits my team had picked out for her but that didn't really help matters much as she wandered around my home wearing the smallest white bikini known to man. I could practically trace the shape of her areola; the triangles of the top were that tiny. Don't even get me started on the bottoms. I stayed indoors all day, hiding out in my office like some scared child as I worked on cases and tried to schedule a meeting with the elusive Lev Volkov. Unfortunately, Rosie seemed to catch me every time I emerged to grab some food or to stretch my legs. It was like she was waiting outside my door just so she could wander past in her almost naked glory.

Today she's in my kitchen, cooking up a storm

wearing nothing but one of my dress shirts. I almost had a heart attack when I saw her, buttons partially undone with the sleeves rolled up to her elbows with cake batter smeared near her tits. Her messy blonde hair was piled up on top of her head, held in place with a chopstick she'd pulled from one of my drawers. She laughed when I'd turned on my heel and walked straight back out of the kitchen, that crazy witch was fucking with me and I was torn between enjoying the push and pull and wanting to put my foot down. It was ridiculous feeling like a horny teenage boy in my own house. Plus, I was getting fucking sick of cold showers and desperate hand jobs.

Settling back at my desk, I reply to an email from Lev requesting that I meet with Alexi and Anoushka, his oldest children instead as he is currently out of the country. Frustrated, I reply, adding a comment about how I hope this isn't an indication of a disruption or issue with our trade routes that I should be aware of. All professionally worded of course.

Hours later Elijah storms into my home office, his dark eyes burning as he slaps his hands down on my desk, leans in and glares at me. "There's a dead Queen in your kitchen making banana muffins, care to explain?"

Fuck. Elijah. He'd been busy investigating potential culprits behind the St Mary's fire, while also sending his men out to dig around The Cartel a little. Our trade routes for White Rabbit were also being re-established and we were introducing a pill form. It had been all hands-on deck and he'd been my representative, while I worked from home. The others probably assumed that the Queen of Hearts had injured me somehow when I'd taken her out. Let them think that. Let them assume I was hiding away licking my wounds, because that was when they would get arrogant and slip up.

With all of that, as well as trying to maintain my public persona, I hadn't managed to tell him about Rosie yet. A part of me also recognized that I might have been avoiding it too, because I knew he'd hold a grudge about the poisoning thing. Eli the man would admire her, Creed, my bodyguard and Left Hand would hate her for beating him.

I sit back in my chair and offer up a small smile. "I wondered what smells so amazing."

I liked banana muffins, I wondered if she'd bring some here later. When she made carrot cake yesterday evening, she knocked on my door while it was still warm. Say what you like about the killer Queen, her baking skills were unmatched. It made me think of my mother's cooking, taking me back to the only good bits of my childhood. I'd never been a skilled chef, it was 'women's work' according to my father. But whenever he was away for business or working late, we'd send the staff home and prepare dinner together. I remember one night, I'd found a radio in one of the cupboards, tidied away by the cook most likely, and I'd brought it out. We'd danced as we washed and peeled potatoes, laughed as she'd added butter and cream and I'd mashed them and when we finally sat down to eat at the kitchen island, I'd felt more at peace than I had in a while. I knew it couldn't last. It never did. We never danced in the kitchen together again after that night.

"Jules!" Elijah hisses, bringing me out of the memories threatening to drown me. "Why aren't you taking this more seriously? The woman who wants you dead is living in your house? Walking around half-naked?"

He rubs his face with his hand, letting out a frustrated groan before throwing himself down on my sofa. I had wondered if he'd say anything about her lack of clothing. It's not like we were fucking, not that the thought hadn't crossed my mind a million times already. Especially at night when I could hear her pleasuring herself. I'm convinced she called out my name as she came last night.

"I have asked her to put some clothes on..."

"You asked her? For fuck's sake Julian. That banshee would cut your throat in your sleep if she could and you're trying to be polite to her?" Elijah scowls at me like I don't understand the position I'm in. I do. I just can't do anything about it. "That harridan stabbed me in the fucking neck. Stabbed. Me. Tell her to put some damn clothes on before I bundle her up in that ugly ass rug you have in the guest room."

"I think she's having fun being here." I shrug. "Yeah that rug is a little...bold."

I heard her singing in the shower this morning and it shouldn't, but it made my house feel a little less empty. A little less lonely. I get glimpses into what our life should have been, if we had been different people and I'm clutching on to it, desperately savoring the moments even though I know they're toxic, rotting me from the inside out.

"Having fun? Having fucking fun? This isn't a slumber party! Someone wants you both dead and I'm almost inclined to let them kill you. Maybe then you'll see some fucking sense." He puts his boots up on my table with a thud, an indicator that he's really pissed off with me because he knows how much it annoys me. He also knows I won't do anything about it. Yet.

Throwing his head back, he stares up at my ceiling, neck tattoos on full display as his long hair falls back. "And how have you only now noticed the fucking rug, man?"

I cough, trying to hide my face behind my hand. "I may be staying in the guest room..."

"You 'may be' staying in the guest bedroom, in your own house?" Eli laughs, and then lights a cigarette. Taking a long pull, he exhales slowly, before pointing it in my direction. "You are so royally fucked, my friend."

The timer for the oven interrupts us, followed by Rosie cursing. Thinking she must have burnt her muffins or touched something hot, I stand. Eli laughs again and I stay where I am, awkwardly pretending to stretch my legs.

Logically, if I let her leave my house now, then she would pose an even bigger risk since she'd gotten a glimpse into my personal life. She'd probably catalogued every way to break in already.

Glancing out of the window, and into the gardens, I notice that my rose bushes are just beginning to bloom and I make a note to show Rosie later. Her garden had always been filled with roses, her mother creating beautiful bouquets and centerpieces out of them for Family events. She'd even brought my mother some one year, for her birthday. Pale yellow roses mixed in with lilacs and baby's breath. Innocence, sincerity and purity. I remembered thinking, *'how delicate...'* as my father had thrown them into the fire, joking about how they were only grown to cover the stench of the dead bodies buried at the Gambino house. He'd suspected for a long time that Vincent was using Rosie to carry out his dirty work, often commenting on how she had no friends, and was too perfect. The only perfect people in the world were cold blooded killers, that's what he'd spit when he was half a bottle of whiskey down. One day, when Rosie trusts me a little more, I'll ask her about it. About how many corpses sat under the soil of her beloved mother's garden and how many she'd killed herself. I wouldn't ask if she felt remorse, because I knew she didn't.

"The pair of you deserve to ruin each other," Elijah grumbles, blowing smoke rings up to my ceiling, grunting every time he glances at me.

"Knock, knock! I bring baked goods and great company!" a cheery voice calls as Elijah makes a disapproving noise and glowers at me, his scar crumpling slightly as he frowns.

She practically dances into the room, like some sort of baking fairy, with a plate of still steaming muffins. I never thought I'd see Rosie Gambino looking like a domestic goddess, but here she is with her blonde hair still pinned up with that solitary chopstick, which Eli eyes wearily, my shirt and bare feet. There's a flour smudge on her flushed cheek as she comes to stand next to me, and as she places the plate down bending across my desk to offer them to Elijah, she gives me a glimpse of everything. It's like my body freezes and I don't know what to say or where to look as the air is sucked out of my lungs violently.

Her glistening pink pussy is presented to me, as she reaches across, her ass so fucking bitable as she practically shoves it in my face. She's wet. She wants me. And I want to bury my face between her folds, devouring her until she begged for mercy. When I was satisfied, and only then, I'd spank her, turning each cheek a bright, furious red for her insubordination.

Glancing over her shoulder at me, Rosie winks. She's playing with me again and I'm so close to snapping. Does she actually want me to fuck her on the desk? Because I will, Eli be damned. He can have a muffin and a show.

With a coy smile, she leaves and closes the door

behind her. I swallow, suddenly able to breathe again and run a hand through my hair, maybe this was a stupid decision. Elijah is right, I'm in too deep and the worst thing about it is how aware I am of the whole situation. Rosie was like an addiction. She was like tooth decay, ruining everything at the root and yet...I hesitated to remove the tooth despite the pain.

Elijah coughs as he stubs out his smoke, bringing me back to the room. "She just showed you her cookies, didn't she?"

I ignore his little baking joke and the way his eyes glint mischievously. "Yep."

He shakes his head. "No panties?"

The word gets lodged in my throat. "Nope."

Laughing he peels the paper wrapper off a muffin and takes a huge bite, before wagging a finger at me. "She'll be the death of you..."

I know.

I know.

I know.

"Tsk. Put your eyes back in your head." His lip curls before he devours the rest of the baked treat the Queen of Hearts offered us with a smile while making herself right at home in her enemy's lair. It was all just a game to her, a petty ruse, a way to rile me up and make me weak. This was a power play. And I was already the loser.

Elijah spends the remainder of the afternoon explaining how my office building was being watched, which means that there was someone on the inside who'd known that we had taken Rosalyn there first and not to one of the other interrogation spaces.

"I've got my men working on it and we'll have the rat soon enough," Elijah grinds out, and I know he'll get the issue resolved. We had a traitor amongst us and it wasn't the chaotic blonde singing loudly in my kitchen as she made something else. Something with cherries, as the dark sinful smell lingered around my house.

"I've found a new informant; they call themselves The Jabberwocky. They think they might be able to get us some valuable intel on The Cartel and their next moves."

When Elijah doesn't make any indication he's joking, I chuckle and take a bite out of another muffin. "Well, we've got a Queen of Hearts in my kitchen and our business ventures come under the WunderLnd Corporation, so why the fuck not?"

Eli's mouth pulls up into a shit eating grin. "Did you see the gossip columns last week? That reporter

Staddon is out there calling the Volkov twins Twee-dledumb and Tweedledee."

He wasn't the biggest fan of the Volkov twins after Anoushka had refused his charming offer to fuck, despite Alexi being more than eager to take his sister's place.

Handing me a file, his face gets serious once again and he gives me a solemn expression. "One of our Captains is also reporting an increase in arrests, now normally if it was someone like Lawrence, then I'd say it's a case of him not looking after his boys properly. But..."

"Who?" Lawrence was famous for blaming everyone but himself, and so if you got caught on a job or doing something a little shady, you were on your own until it was brought to my attention. Then it was my role, as either the head of The Family or as a prac-ticing lawyer to fix it. If I couldn't, we sent in Eli with less traditional methods.

"Nicco and I looked into it. The Judge sending them to the clink is Joseph Walters."

"The one with the moustache? Who looks like a walrus?" I hated Judge Walters, he was always overly harsh with his sentencing and spoke to everyone beneath him like shit. It was all ironic, considering a little birdie told me his son was dying to become one of our club designated dealers. "He's clearly got some sort of vendetta, do a little more digging."

"Is that all?" I want to lay my head on my desk and sleep. It felt like everything was one good hard pull from unweaving, and the tapestry I'd dedicated my life to was about to become nothing but loose threads.

Standing, Eli stretches, obviously feeling as exhausted as I do, if not more since he actually had to do the grunt work. He shows me a series of messages from the manager at the gentleman's club downtown. "The Top Hat have reported suspicious people from Aberfalls making enquiries about one of their dancers. Rich, entitled shitheads apparently. Claiming she's family. They've been barred, but Lilith is concerned."

I rub my temples and reach for another muffin, only stopping when Eli's eyebrow arches. "Is she underage?"

"No."

I get to my feet and escort him to the front door. "Then we tell them nothing. We protect our own, from the cleaners and dancers, to the assholes who sit at my table. Give her time off, fully paid, and set up extra security at the club."

"Understood." He pulls me into a quick hug, patting my back. "Are you sure you don't need me to stay the night?"

He doesn't think I can be trusted here alone with Rosie since she was obviously trying to escalate the situation between us, moving on from jerk-off sessions to something a little more hands on but Elijah couldn't stop me if I decided to fuck Rosie, no one could. She was mine.

"I'll be fine," I say with a chuckle. I'm a grown man, a local celebrity, a hotshot lawyer, the head of a mafia organization and he was worried about what? My virtue? I'd never had any to begin with.

Shaking his head, he sighs, "No, you won't."

———

The second the front door clicks shut and I turn the lock, I know I'm in danger. I can feel it in my bones, this awareness of her. I try to head up the stairs without making a sound, creeping around in my own house but all the noise in the kitchen suddenly goes quiet.

"Julian? Are you running away from me?" she sings out, her accusatory tone carrying through the large empty building. All the staff had either retired for the day or left the property, meaning there was only the two of us once again.

"No, I'm just tired," I say, taking another step. It

wasn't exactly a lie. It had been incredibly draining in my office with Eli. The problems were like weeds, and I was ripping them up, only to have two more sprout beneath my feet. I'm almost at the top of the stairs now, so close to being able to take a cold shower and get the image of her perfect pussy out of my head. It was hell having a woman I was supposed to hate, a woman who wanted to destroy me, taunting me in my home like I was her plaything.

"Oh." Is it my imagination or does she sound disappointed? Whatever it is, it doesn't last long as her soft feminine voice teases, "Too tired to hear about my mole in your building?"

I pause. "I'm sorry...what?"

Is she lying to get my attention? No, she would just walk around naked for that. How did she get anyone past Elijah? All of our staff were either extensively vetted, or they were part of The Family, in which case they knew the punishment for betrayal. The Gambino's were a bloody reminder that still shook our community, ten years later.

She's standing in the doorway to my kitchen, with a mixing bowl against her hip, leaning against the frame as she watches me. The light coming from behind her means that the shirt is almost useless, the white fabric sheer as I can make out every curve of her silhouette.

Stirring her mixture, she licks the spatula before casually saying, "You aren't the only one who sent spies over the years Jay. Let's just say we both clearly like watching one another too much for it to be healthy."

So that's how she knew about White Rabbit and the supplier issues we were having, she was spying on me. Infiltrating my life, even though I'd been careful. Nothing about our dynamic was healthy. She was playing games with me again. Sucking me in, before she spat me out, just like at our dinner disaster a few weeks ago.

"Tell me what you know," I demand.

"No." Another slow lick of the spoon.

My dick twitches and internally I curse. "Tell me."

"No, you'll have to torture me for that information. Or beg. I haven't decided which yet." Her expression is thoughtful for a moment, as if she's picturing me on my knees before her. That's when I decided that if this was going to happen, it was going to happen on my terms.

"You'd like that, wouldn't you," I murmur as I take each step at a leisurely pace.

As I reach the bottom, she retreats into the kitchen

a little, eyes narrowed as her whole body goes on alert. The Queen of Hearts is on the backfoot, only for a moment but it's enough as I saunter towards her.

"What?" she stammers, stepping back again.

"Torture for information," I say nonchalantly, with a shrug. It turns out that while old Vincent Gambino was making his daughter a killer Queen, he forgot to factor in how much she liked it. That's why she was so good at being the bloodthirsty bitch everyone knew her as, because she was practically begging to be fucked every time anyone was rough with her. Getting violent made her horny, and I planned to use that to my advantage.

"Don't think I haven't noticed how it gets you off every time we fight." She enjoyed the power, because she always knew she'd win, but not this time. I had finally found a way to break Rosalyn Gambino and it wasn't with a gun or a knife, although she'd probably enjoy that too. "Are you trying to provoke me into manhandling you? Bending you over my knee?"

"I don't know what you're talking about." She turns towards the oven, pretending to check the temperature settings as she twiddles with some buttons. Her cheeks are flushed as she stirs whatever mix is in the bowl again.

I tut, taking the stupid bowl from her hands, and

invade her space to place it on the island counter. Reaching behind her means I've boxed her in between my arms, as I lean in and whisper, "I thought we agreed not to lie to each other in this house."

There's something about my words that spark more intimacy than it should. This house. Almost like it was our house.

She rolls her eyes as I stay where I am, almost pressed up against her. "Besides I only have to wrap my hands around like this..." My fingers slide across the column of her neck before I hold her in a firm grip, "To test my theory."

Her breath hitches but she doesn't move away, her big blue eyes, swirled through with grey and gold specks, watching me intensely. Her hands tremble by her sides as she struggles with the urge to push me away. She's been taught to fight, to always be in control, but like this she's vulnerable.

"Let's try this again," I say, squeezing as I brush my lips against her ear. "Who is the rat?"

She shakes her head, but I see the corner of her mouth lift upwards. I tighten my grip, feeling her swallow beneath my palm as I do. She was still passive in my hands, letting me dominate her.

"Give me what I want," I growl.

She laughs, well as much as my hold will allow. "I'm all yours, baby."

I bite the fleshy part of her ear. "Information Rosie, I want information."

"What do I get in return?" she croaks, as she moves her hips closer to me.

I ask a dangerous question, knowing that there is no going back from whatever her answer may be. "What do you want?"

Chapter Fourteen

Rosie

What do I want?

> Power?
> Money?
> The Family?

Everything he owns?

Yes. I do.

But not at this moment. At this moment, when we're pressed up against his kitchen island, with his hand around my neck like he owns me, I only want him. I want him to consume me, to gobble me up like I'm a pecan pie. There's so much left unspoken between us, so much history that becomes this tangible, palpable tension that seems to take over my brain whenever I'm around him. I'm losing to Julian Asaro and I'm not even going to bat an eyelid because I can get back on top another night. Tonight, I want to be under him, like it's my life's mission.

"You. Inside me. Now." I moan as I grind against him. I can feel him chuckle as he kisses my forehead. He loves the power he has over me, we both know it. I quickly unbutton the shirt I stole from his wardrobe and shrug it to the floor so that I'm completely exposed, my skin pebbling in the cool kitchen.

Jay says nothing, but I can feel him inhale slowly as he looks at me with a hungry gaze. He swallows, his Adam's apple bobbing and it seems like I'm not the only one with a tenuous hold on their control right now.

Softly he presses his lips against mine, it's not enough to be a kiss, it's a tease as he moves away. His free hand skims the curve of my body as it moves lower. Running his fingers along my slit he asks, "Like this?"

Sliding two fingers inside me, he keeps me in place with his hand around my neck.

I can't help the mewling noise that escapes my mouth, "Mmmm."

He cuts off the sound with his lips, but that doesn't completely silence me. He just devours my lust. I'm not a virgin, not in a million years . . . but this was Julian. Everything felt amplified. Everything was dripping in anticipation and emotion, hate, anger, love, lust and pain. It was merging into one as he overtook my senses with a kiss that I felt all the way to my core.

He begins to move his thumb slowly over my clit, my body swaying as he tightens his grip and cuts down my air supply as he teases me. Breaking from our kiss, he smirks. "Or do you want something more?"

I whimper, feeling a little ashamed of the noises I'm making. The one and only Queen of Hearts is a whimpering mess at the hands of her enemy.

"Then give me the name Rosalyn."

I shake my head and almost shout as he withdraws his fingers and lets go of my throat. Grabbing my ass roughly, kneading the skin in his hands, grinding his hard-on against me. Fuck. He's huge. And I want him but I'm not ready to give him what he wants, not just yet. I make quick work of the buttons on his shirt and my mouth practically waters as I watch him discard it.

"Now," he commands but again I shake my head as he lifts my leg, fingers digging into my thigh as he grinds against my clit. The rough texture of his trousers against my sensitive flesh drives me crazy, why are there still clothes between us?

"Last chance," Jay warns as he unbuttons his trousers and pushes them down one-handed. We both know what he's threatening to do, he is going to get naked, take me to the edge and then leave me unsatisfied and angry. He's giving me a taste of my own medicine, it's payback from the dinner where I promised everything and gave him nothing.

He pinches my nipple between his fingers, twisting and squeezing as he burns me with his gaze. I want more. It's not enough. It was never going to be enough and I should have known that.

"Daniel." I groan as I tilt my head back, I may just come from the friction of the dry humping if he carries on.

"No," Jay's voice is firm. "He's loyal to me."

I can't resist taunting Julian, his little Family is nothing but an empty palace, filled with squabbling old men, built upon a sandy shore, where the foundations are just as weak as the turrets at the top.

I'd met Daniel by chance, at The Gryphon a year or so after Belcastro's death. I'd gone with Cato, looking to make some extra money and do a little digging on Jay, gauge how his men felt about his unprecedented rise to power. There was hierarchy and order within

The Family, and yet Frank had ignored all of that and placed Julian at the top of the chain. Why?

There wasn't an official dress code at The Gryphon, but Cato and I had dressed up since they would be recognized as a 'designated dealer'. We'd both worn cute black filigree lace masks, tied up with ribbon and while Cato had paired theirs with a short black dress and thigh-high boots. I'd worn trousers and a blazer with only my red bra underneath. The crowd that night had been a mix of Newtown's elite and wealthy, rubbing shoulders with some of the lower classes. Anyone who cleared the background checks, and had money to burn was welcomed at the underground fighting hall.

It wasn't until one guy decided to get a little handsy with me during the fight, grabbing my ass and trying to pull me into his lap that my patience with the loud, leery crowd started to wane. When his fat, furry tongue licked the curve of my neck and he tried to suck my earlobe between his practically toothless gums, I finally lost my cool. I'd grabbed his tongue between my thumb and my forefinger, pulled my blade from my boot and sliced the offending appendage clean off. I tossed the useless muscle onto the sticky, blood-spattered, beer-stained floor, ignoring the man's wails as I stood and left.

No one had even noticed, the rowdy crowd cheering as the fight drew to a bloody conclusion. Except Daniel. He looked up at me with those big sad, brown eyes of his from across the room and I knew he'd seen the entire thing. With a grin, I'd winked and walked away, thinking I'd never see him again. He followed me into an alleyway a week later, and with my gun pressed against his forehead, proceeded to tell me how much he admired me, and how he thought I should have been the head of The Family. He wanted to help me claim what should have been 'rightfully mine'.

His words were pure flattery. The Family was a patriarchal construct that had never been 'rightfully mine', but I had intended to make it mine, even if I had to fight tooth and nail for it. I humored him, told him I appreciated his support and that's when he told me he had an interview to be Julian's personal assistant. He was my way in. It was that easy.

"Loyalty is a fickle thing Jay, it can be bought or traded." Grabbing a handful of his hair, I yank his head backwards, enjoying the suspicion and torment that flashes across his face. The fact that I'd had someone who was that close to him, watching him for years is a cruel reminder of who I am and what this is between us.

"What did he want? How did you get to him?" He snarls, thrusting his cock harder against me, moving across my clit in a way that has my toes curling.

"Stop trying to edge me Jay..." I taste the dip at the bottom of his throat, swirling my tongue over the hot skin.

"Answer the questions, Rosie. You want your orgasm?" His hand returns to my neck, where it belongs, and he uses his thumb to apply pressure, making my head go light. "Earn it."

"He wants to fuck me." Licking my lips, I buck my hips against his hardness, I'm so close. I'm almost there. Almost... "Be my King."

Jay stills as I whine, a dark glint in his eyes as he takes in the sight of me, completely exposed and vulnerable to him as he still holds my leg. Jealousy is a good look on him, and it makes me want to run my hands over his chest, so I do, leaving long, raw red marks on his skin. Marking him as mine.

Fisting a hand in my hair, he growls as he pulls my head back. "I'm your King."

With a smirk, I whisper, "Prove it."

My words do the trick, like I knew they would. Julian pulls me off the counter and turns me around so that my ass is exposed to him.

"You asked for this. Don't forget that," he reminds

me before reaching across and grabbing the spatula from my mixing bowl. With a hard *whack* that echoes around the room, he spanks me, not holding anything back. I can feel the wet cake batter against my hot skin as the pain registers. His words are to keep me anchored, so that I don't unleash my instincts to fight but he needn't have worried. I enjoy the bite of the silicone against my ass

He lightly rubs the skin, before landing another swat on my backside. *Whack*. This one is harder and there's something delicious about the way my skin burns long after he's removed his hand. *Whack*.

Whack. The final slap makes me groan and tiptoe so that my ass is higher in the air for him. I can almost feel him smiling even though I can't see his face. I've pressed my cheek against the cool marble of the work-top, watching him. Julian Asaro is a man who never loses his cool, he's always calm and collected. His rationality is what makes him a strategist, a thinker rather than a doer, like me. With his hair mussed, cheeks flushed, beautiful body covered in my marks and a wild look in his eyes, the man standing behind me is not the same Julian the rest of the world knows. This is Jay.

Tossing the spatula back into the bowl, he stands back to admire his handiwork. Bending down, he licks the long stripes of cake batter from my skin, his tongue hot, wet and soothing against my raw backside.

Finally, he parts my legs a little and presses himself against my opening. He teases me again, brushing over my clit mercilessly, as his cock slides through the wetness gathered between my legs. No one had ever made me as wet as Jay had tonight, and he hadn't even fucked me yet.

Grabbing my hair, he pulls me back into his chest and kisses me. This isn't like the others; this is him showing me that he owns my body as his tongue invades my mouth. I can barely think as he dominates my lips, sucking, biting, licking anything and everything his mouth touches. His other hand snakes around my body to cup my breast and as he rolls my nipple between his fingers, he slides inside me. It takes me a second to adjust to the size of him and I realize that's why he distracted me. He begins to flex his hips, moving slowly in and out of my soaking wet pussy. There are no better words to describe it, because right now it feels like I'm the star in a porno. My body begins to anticipate each thrust, clenching and tightening every time he slides into me and I can feel my orgasm building within minutes.

"Whose cock is inside you right now?" he

murmurs into my ear, sending a burst of pleasure down my spine.

"Yours," I breathe, teetering on the edge of an abyss.

"And how do you feel now? Still empty?" This man was becoming obsessed with my feelings as if he was responsible for them, and I don't know why, but I liked the idea of that.

"No. So...fucking...full."

Smack! Another slap lands on my ass and the guttural noises I'm making fill the kitchen as he fucks me slowly, taking his sweet time. "Who's your King, Rosie?"

I bite my lip as it feels like a wave building inside me. My body is slick with sweat as he's worked me up into a horny frenzy, all my nerves frayed and firing after the teasing and torture. Julian was foreplay on a plate and I'd been feasting myself on him since this afternoon, when I had shown him what was on offer.

Pinching my nipple, he demands, "Answer me. Who. Is. Your. King?"

It's the easiest question in the world. Every word punctuated with the thrust of his hips. "You are."

His hand slides from my hair down my body to my clit, where his fingertips push me over the edge. My legs threaten to buckle as my orgasm washes over me, my body not feeling like mine anymore. He thrusts a few more times, prolonging the ecstasy just a little longer before his grip on my tit tightens and I know he's about to shoot his load.

"Mine," he hisses against my shoulder with his final thrust. I feel warmth as he paints my insides with his cum, his fingers biting into my skin with every little aborted hip-thrust.

Once he's satisfied, he pulls out slowly and places his palm on the bottom of my back, pushing me gently back down onto the counter. Taking two fingers, he scoops up the cum that's started to trail down my thighs, and pushes it back inside me with a possessive grunt.

"Mine," he hisses once again, my chest tightening as the word brushes over my skin.

I don't correct him.

I don't want to.

I'll deal with that when the sun rises.

J ulian leads me upstairs into my room, bundles me into the shower, pinning me to the tiles as he lifts me. I wrap my legs around his hips and without a single word spoken between us, he fucks me again.

The way he thrusts into me is wild, without abandon as if he can't get enough, mouth biting at my skin, fingers pinching and dragging as he tries to devour me once again. All his frustration and anger flows between us, as I call out his name, lost in waves of pleasure and pain.

He comes, filling me up like it was his life's mission to pump so much cum into me that it started spilling out of my mouth. He held us in place against the wall, forehead against mine as his breathing returned to normal. After a few minutes, he lowers me down carefully, and does something unexpected. He washes my hair, carefully shampoo and conditioning it, before washing my body tenderly.

When we leave the bathroom, he wraps an arm around my waist. "Your turn."

"Hmmm?" I reply, sleepily after being railed twice and having the most amazing shower.

With a grin, he tosses me on the bed and pulls away my towel. Parting my legs, he kisses up my thighs and gives me the second-best orgasm of my life, ripping it from me as I scream his name and clamp my legs around his head. Afterwards, he tucks me under the covers and slides into the bed beside me. Curling his big, warm body around mine, he holds me firmly against him as he drifts to sleep.

Once Julian is snoring softly, I untangle myself from him and make my way downstairs, being careful not to disturb him. When I first arrived here, he had confiscated all my belongings, apparently for his safety and to continue the ruse that he'd killed me, but there were still some calls I needed to make. And one person who needed to know that I was still very much alive.

Yesterday, I'd managed to swipe the gardener's phone when I was talking to him about the roses planted near the pool, it didn't require skill, simply nimble fingers and a sweet smile. Afterwards I tucked it away in a plant pot in the main lounge, waiting for a quiet moment where I could use it. With Jay upstairs, worn out from the multiple rounds of sex and working out some of our aggression towards one another, there wasn't likely to be a better opportunity.

Like always, my heart thumps in my chest, every bad thing that could have happened running through my mind as I wait for her to pick up. The phone rings five times before she answers and I exhale with relief.

"Gunpowder. Gelatin. Dynamite," I say, keeping my voice low as I curl up on the sofa with my legs beneath me, a single lamp casting out a dim glow in the room. We'd established code words and phrases for situations like this, it was just a way to ensure we were safe and free to talk if we'd been separated for more than two days.

"Hmmmm, guaranteed to blow your freaking mind," a sleepy voice replies, before Lola yawns. "Oh, you're still alive then?"

I snort softly, looking around the luxurious room I was currently hiding in. I wasn't just alive; I was living in absolute heaven. "Of course I am."

I can hear her rustling around, getting out of bed on the other end of the line. I could just imagine her, padding to her kitchen in her pajamas to grab a bottle of flavored water from her fridge before curling up on her loveseat. "He hasn't killed you yet then?"

"Obviously," I drawl, doing a Snape impression. Twisting a curl in between my fingers, I groan. "There's more than one way to die, Lola."

Silence down the line.

Lola sniggers, "You totally fucked him, didn't you?"

"He fucked me, thoroughly." I sigh dramatically, wiggling in my seat as I feel the burn between my legs and bruises on my skin from his fingertips.

"That sounds like dangerous territory Ro," Lola's voice softens, and I know she's worried that I'm in over my head. She's always worried when it comes to Julian. She seems to think he's my Achilles heel or something.

There's more silence, this time mine. And I know there's a million things happening in those spaces. Words that should be said. Words that can't be said. Words that hurt.

Eventually, I exhale. "I know."

"Want to talk about it?"

Looking down at the shirt I'm wearing, a loose thread catches my eye and I pull on it. I tug and tug at it until more of it unravels. "No, what's the point? Once he finds Daniel and we find out who's trying to frame me, I'm out of here. I'll probably have to lay low for a while again. But that's nothing new."

On the move again. Sofa surfing. Relying on my connections, my reputation or my body for a safe place to stay. It used to be exciting, I used to feel like I was being a genius, outsmarting Jay at every turn. Now it felt like I was running away.

Lola must sense the dip in my mood as she

changes tactics. "What's it like there then? His house?"

Glancing around the large room again, there's an ache I don't want to acknowledge. Instead, I start bragging, focusing on the silver linings of this little kidnapping. "It's like an all-inclusive holiday! I have free reign of his mansion and all the surrounding grounds. He has a pool, beautiful garden and Lola, the kitchen is amazing. It's fully stocked and all I've done is bake, swim and fuck."

She sighs, "Sounds perfect."

"Yeah." It does. There's that ache again.

"Well, at least when you leave, Julian will be fifty pounds heavier and completely enthralled with your pussy." She chuckles, and stifles a yawn. Glancing at the clock above the fireplace, I can see it's almost 4am, and Julian had to be up at six most days.

"Mmm. Are you and Cato alright?"

With my death being spread through The Family, I worried about them. We tried to keep our friendship hidden, meeting in private spaces or crowded ones like The Blue Caterpillar where we could hide in plain sight, but nothing was ever truly safe, not when there was a bounty on your head.

"I haven't seen or heard from them." There's a pause before Lola speaks again, sounding nervous.

"I've been thinking, I might leave town for a while, just a little bit."

I stiffen. "Is everything okay? It's not the stalker, is it?"

"Yeah, my past has just come knocking finally and it's time to deal with it. Y'know? It's nothing to do with Dante."

"Ooooh, Dante?" I tease. Swallowing, I try to hide the worry I can feel unfurling in the pit of my stomach. Lola was a badass, like me. She could handle herself and a gun but that didn't mean I didn't worry about her. If she was telling me like this, instead of just dealing with it and then catching me up on the details later, it meant she thought there was a possibility she might not come back to Newtown. Or back to me. Closing my eyes, I tilt my head backwards, letting a tear run silently down my cheek. "Be safe."

"Always."

Chapter Fifteen

Julian

I wake in my bed to find Rosie on her knees between my legs. She's completely naked, her blonde curls a messy halo around her head as she places a lazy kiss on my thigh, near one of my scars. She's got my cock in her hands, and it's already hard. Her mouth turns up into a sly grin as she realizes I'm awake.

"Where is the blanket?" I ask as I come around. I have never been a morning person but seeing Rosie's tits near my dick while her ass is in the air is a hell of a way to wake up.

"On the floor." She shrugs as she moves her fist up

the length of my dick, we both watch the bead of pre-cum forming on the head.

"What are you doing?" I ask as if it isn't obvious. She wants to play again this morning, but for how long until she decides to kill me? I thought I could handle one taste of Rosie, one night, maybe even try to use sex to tame her but yesterday proved that I couldn't be trusted when it came to Rosalyn. I wanted more. Craved her more. And while she was playing along for now, acting like she was desperate for this too, I would be the one broken in the end.

"Paying tribute to my King." As she drags out the word 'king' she flicks her tongue over the tip of my cock, making it twitch beneath her touch. She takes as much of me as she can into her mouth and sucks, hollowing out her cheeks before moving up and down on my cock like a woman desperate to taste me. I weave my hands through her hair and I don't miss the way she hums in approval. Taking her lead, I force her down a little harder on my dick. She gags, eyes watering but she quickly adjusts as I start moving my hips upwards to match her movements. She hums again, making throaty sounds that send vibrations down my cock and make my balls clench.

Her legs part and from where I'm lying, I see her hand disappear between her legs as she brings me to the brink of losing control. Why did she have this effect on me?

"Stop," I commanded, my voice heavy with lust. She pulls away, looking a little sad.

"Why? Don't you want to come in my mouth?" Rosie pouts, as if I'm denying her something instead of myself.

"Yes. A million times, yes. But right now, I want to come inside you." My words bring back her smile as she crawls up my body and slides herself onto me. She really didn't need to be told twice, and the noise she makes as she lowers herself fully onto me almost makes me come then and there. Why her? Why did it have to be Rosie who made me feel like this? My mind blanks when she's fully seated, and all I can feel is her hot, tight body wrapped around mine.

She moves slowly at first, and it's mesmerizing watching the way her hips roll as she brings us both pleasure.

Placing her hands on my chest, she leans in and kisses me, her taste heady and intoxicating as she dominates every corner, every crevice of my being. Lifting her hips, she drops herself down onto my length in short bursts, tight pussy milking me as I thrust up into her.

Leaning back with her hands now resting on my

thighs, she writhes and squirms on top of me, taking what she needs from me as she pushes us towards the edge of insanity. My fingers dig into her hips and she smirks before running her hands through her hair, giving me the most amazing view of her tits as they bounce.

"You keep coming inside me like this and you're going to get me pregnant," she teases as she moves a little faster, skin slick with sweat as she works me over.

For some reason, the animal part of my brain likes the idea of filling her up, of making her body round and heavy with my baby. She would be mine. I reach up and squeeze her tits before teasing her nipples. "I don't care."

She falters for a moment before continuing, harder and faster than before. "Don't forget who we are, Julian."

Her words bite, I haven't forgotten, but the lines are so blurred right now as she rides me like I'm a fucking prized pony. It doesn't take long for either of us to come, her orgasm first, and as she comes down from the high, her body clenching around mine, finishes me off. This is what sex should be like. Intense. Intoxicating. Never enough.

She leans forward and rests her head on my sweaty chest. "Want to shower together?"

"Of course, I do."

"So, you went there then?" Elijah asks as he sits at my kitchen table and helps himself to the stack of pancakes Rosie put out five minutes ago along with the fresh coffee. He'd let himself into the house just after nine, loudly. Calling out and making lots of noise as if he was scared he was going to catch us fucking in the hallway.

"I don't know what you mean," I say, reading the newspaper and ignoring his glares.

He's got his long hair tied up today, and he's wearing a fitted black T-shirt, black combat trousers and a pair of black boots, which means he likely rode his bike over here rather than driving his car. He looks tired, and agitated, not that I blame him. It had been past midnight when I had the opportunity to text him about Daniel, and ask him to look deeper into Rosie's claims.

She seems oblivious to his sharp looks, as she dances around the kitchen to the radio while making something else that smells divine, wearing one of my

T-shirts and a pair of pajama trousers that are far too long on her but she's rolled them up in an attempt to make it work. I haven't had a breakfast this domestic in a while...if ever.

Elijah shovels another mouthful in. "She's humming and you're avoiding looking at her when yesterday you couldn't tear your eyes away. Pussy. Whipped."

If it had been anyone else, I would have snapped at the impertinence. But this was Eli, my childhood friend. I still wasn't going to let him make me feel embarrassed, despite the way I can feel the tips of my ears heat.

"Did you find Daniel?" I ask, swiftly changing the subject.

Daniel was my employee for over three years, how could he betray me? I watch as she places fresh croissants on the table, okay...I can see how you'd be tempted but he'd been through a lot by my side. That should have counted for something. Loyalty used to mean something. Rosie was more loyal to me, and she wanted to rip everything out from under my feet. At least she was honest with it, I think bitterly.

"Yes," Elijah growls as he tears open a French pastry and smears jam over it. "Little fucking rat was hiding out in the cellar of a strip club. Family owned."

I know he was feeling just as betrayed as I was. How many situations had we been in together, the three of us? How many times had I put my trust in him? Told him things that were confidential or sought out his opinion?

Rosie takes the seat next to me, a cup of tea in her hand. "Oh, Paulie's?"

"Yeah," Elijah replies, eyes narrowed as he glares a hole into the side of her face.

Shrugging, she gives me a small smile.

"Of course." Elijah tosses his croissant back down onto the plate with a frustrated grunt, throwing his hand in the air with an eye roll. "Of course, he's one of your supporters."

Rosie sips from her mug and says nothing. Her hair is tied up into a ponytail today and I have to push away thoughts of wrapping her long blonde locks around my hand and dragging her onto the table and making her deep throat me while I stand at the head of the table. She takes another mouthful of her tea and my eyes follow the length of her throat as she swallows. God. How was she having this effect on me?

I look away, and that's when I notice it isn't just me staring at her. Elijah doesn't look at her like he wants to fuck her, but he's definitely not disinterested enough for my taste.

Leaning forward on his elbows, Eli asks, "Do you have a magical cunt? Is that what this is? Everyone just wants to fuck you and if they do, you own their soul?"

Rosie licks her lips as she reaches across the table for some pancakes. Winking at him, she teases, "Why sweetie, want a taste?"

They lock eyes and it's like the room comes to a standstill as the tension crackles in the air. My Left Hand wasn't used to being challenged and the Queen of Hearts was having too much fun taunting him.

She doesn't cave, staring at him like he fascinates her. It was almost beautiful, the expression on her face, except I knew what was really going on in her head. In her mind she was weighing him up, dismantling him piece by piece like he was nothing more than a machine. An obstacle in her life. It was how her father raised her after all, I'd seen his notes on her training when his office had been ransacked in the aftermath. She wasn't just a woman; she was a weapon.

She blows him a kiss and his lip curls in response. "You sure you don't want to?"

Folding my newspaper, I slam it down on the table, relishing the way neither of them flinch, but they both tense. Trained killers wary of me, the arguably weakest player in the room. Good.

My irrational jealousy rears its ugly head as I grab her chin and force her to look at me. "Let's not play with fire before lunchtime, Rosie."

She flutters her eyelashes and sticks out her bottom lip, she was having fun baiting my man and I'd just put my foot down, ruining her entertainment for the morning. The cuteness she's giving me is a mask, and I won't entertain it. "Behave."

She bows her head, submitting to me and that makes my dick hard, even though I know her submission is only temporary while she's a guest in my home.

Eli grins, voice smug and satisfied. "Yeah, Rosie."

Flipping him off before finishing off her tea, she retorts, "Only he can call me Rosie, asshole. It's Rosalyn."

Mimicking her tone, Elijah replies, "Only he can call me Asshole, *Rosalyn*."

Rosie laughs, brandishing a knife as she spreads butter on a croissant. "I think we're going to get on just fine Creed—when you pull that stick out of your ass."

It's only a butter knife, but Elijah had already seen the damage she could do with a poisoned hairpin and while he doesn't shrink back, he does eye her warily. He doesn't trust her, not in a million years and it shows because it's making him nervous.

"I doubt it, Queen of Hearts," he sneers at her, "Unlike Jules, I don't play house with killer Queens."

She shrugs, cheerily, ponytail swinging. "That's because you're a sore loser, who's intimidated by my reputation."

I watch them both with my brows raised, wondering what fucking alternative universe I've landed in this morning where sassy and sarcastic is the main meal of the day. Pulling my phone out of my waistcoat, I fire off a quick message to Anoushka Volkov. I have a favor to ask, and if she wants to keep me happy and ensure I invest in her family's gun trade, she will be more than willing to help me out.

"I highly doubt that, I've probably killed more men than you've had cock." Creed pulls two more pancakes from the stack onto his plate, trailing hot butter everywhere. "And I ain't saying you're a hoe, but I'm willing to bet you've had a lot of dick."

I tense, waiting to see how she'll react. She wanted to play this morning, and if you piss off the Left Hand, this is what you get. Creed isn't like us, he doesn't give a shit about manners or social graces. He does the dirty work because he enjoys not having to reign himself in.

Placing her mug down calmly, Rosie scowls at him. "Spit out the pancake, Creed. I don't feed mouthy little boys who talk trash because they want to puff out their chests and play with the professionals. Spit. It. Out. Before I make you."

"Nope." Eli grins, wiping syrup from the corner of his mouth in a large exaggerated motion.

Before either of us can react, she lunges across the table and punches him square in the throat, forcing him to spit out his mouthful just so he can try and breathe.

As he slams his hands down on the table, face turning puce as he sucks in huge gulping breaths, she snags his whole plate away. "Naughty boys don't get pancakes! Or croissants!"

When he's finally in control of his own respiratory system, he waves his hand at her and glowers at me, as if to say 'What the fuck is this madness? Make it go away!'

"Oh sit down, I did warn you." She rolls her eyes as she crosses her arms.

"And that makes it okay?" he hisses, reaching out for the serving plate of pastries but she's quicker, pushing it out of his reach before his fingertips can even brush the edge of the plate.

"How about a wager, Creed, slayer of many millions of men?" She chuckles to herself. "Starting today we keep a tally. The score gets calculated the next time we run into one another. Winner gets bragging rights; loser shuts the fuck up."

Eli's eyes narrowed into slits as he took his seat again. "You're a forked tongue liar, how will I know if you're telling the truth."

Tilting her head, she looks young and innocent with her large blue eyes and oversized clothing. "You won't."

Grunting, Eli crosses his arms and mimics her pose. "Cheater and a fucking liar, that how you roll *Rosalyn*?"

"Take the wager and I'll let you eat breakfast," she says, tempting him by lifting the plate and giving it a little wiggle.

"Give it a rest, children," I warn as I pour myself another coffee from the carafe brewed earlier. They both watch me, and it feels strange to have them sitting at my table so relaxed. Strange but not uncomfortable. Rosie pushes his plate back towards him in silence before returning to her mug of tea.

"So how are we doing this?" Eli asks as he carries

on stuffing his face and takes a deep inhale of the meat Rosie's slow roasting in the oven.

I don't know why it surprised me, the last few days, to learn that Rosie was obsessed with baking and cooking. Her mother, although not of Italian descent, was very similar to The Family wives in the way she was very hospitable, always making sure everyone had a drink or enough to eat. The Welsh heritage meant she wasn't shy with her measurements or portions either, and as I eye the pile of croissants still left, I wonder if I even own a Tupperware container with a lid. I guess Rosie hadn't been able to spend much time in a kitchen like this over the last ten years, since her family was killed. Revenge isn't really a dish that requires a preheated oven and sprinkles.

A text comes through from the female Volkov twin and I smile, glad that something is going my way for a change.

"The Volkov's are allowing us to use one of their warehouses down at the docks for the interrogation. They say that they've also caught a little rodent of their own they think we might be interested in."

"Two for the price of one?" Eli grins. "How like the Volkov's."

Rosie gets to her feet and loads her mug into the

dishwasher, checking on her beef joint before coming back to the table. "You don't think they're actually fucking, do you?"

I raise my hand to stop Eli answering, since I know what he's going to say anyway. "He's bitter about being turned down by Anoushka, so he'll tell you yes."

"I am not bitter." He huffs, pulling out his phone, likely to tell a few of the men on his security team to meet us down at the docks.

"You could have always taken Alexi home, he likes it rough." Rosie shrugs, turning pink when she catches my unimpressed glare. "Or so I've heard..."

"Lotta dick," Eli coughs, not-so-inconspicuously, whining when I kick him under the table, fed up with his antics.

"Let's be serious about this," I demand, and I tap my fingers against the table. We had never worked together before like this, Rosie and I. We were always playing cat and mouse with one another, but we were never on the same team.

"You should question Daniel first. Then you should let me in," Rosie offers, an earnest expression falling into place. "It will undo Daniel."

To my surprise Elijah nods, as if her plan makes sense, as if it was already the foregone conclusion. Had he already forgotten who the head of this Family is? Or like the others, was he defecting now that she'd managed to beat him twice? I rolled my eyes at my own thoughts, Eli was loyal. I would bet my life on that. But...wouldn't I have said the same for Daniel too only days ago?

"You can't kill him," I say, my voice firm as I remind them who I am. Daniel is my employee. I hired him. I trained him. I trusted him. I was in control here until Rosie stood over my dead body, my crown clenched between her bloody fingers.

"He's a traitor," Rosie states simply and the cool look in her eyes makes the hairs on my arms rise. This. This was the Rosie the others knew. This was the Queen of Hearts, no compassion, no mercy, only revenge and punishment. She sat back and crossed her arms, waiting for my response.

"He betrayed *me*," I remind them both. I understand what he's done if he's guilty. I know what is expected of me if he is a traitor. The rules of The Family were ruthless, we couldn't afford to let people like Daniel get away with spying and disloyalty. Who knows what was compromised or who else he'd exposed or put at risk? "But it should be my decision, because this is my playground and these are my rules."

The corner of Rosie's mouth twitches. "And if he's

behind the shit with the church, he attempted to frame me. I demand retribution."

"I will punish him accordingly," I say calmly, but I don't miss the way she and Elijah share a look, sending a shiver down my spine.

Chapter Sixteen

Rosie

As the sun sets, Creed drives us into the city and towards the docks and the warehouse the Volkov's used to ship their guns. It had been smart thinking on Jay's part to use a facility that wasn't directly tied to The Family, since we were about to interrogate traitors and neither of us knew who to trust any more.

When we locate the warehouse and make our way inside, we're greeted by the very beautiful Volkov twins and two members of security. I'd yet to meet the Volkov's personally before, but I'd been to their club The Blue Butterfly, and their restaurant The Bistro, and I'd always thought the rumors of them being drugged up, sex-crazed party animals were a little far-fetched. Looking at them now, I realized that they'd taken that part of their personalities, and made it their whole public persona. And I didn't like it.

Anoushka Volkov steps forward with a small seductive smile, and hands Creed a set of keys. Her almost white hair is pinned up gracefully, a stark contrast to her fitted black dress and red heels, all very expensive looking. It's easy to see why she used to be a model as she oozes sex appeal naturally, without having to do much other than breathe. When she opens her mouth and her heavily accented Russian comes out, it does nothing to detract from that. In fact, it only seems to make her more charming. *Fuck her.*

"Mr. Asaro, you'll find everything you requested through those doors. If you need any further assistance, please simply let our man Sergei know." She motions over to the two security men who nod in our direction before moving towards the front of the warehouse to give us a little more privacy.

I bite the inside of my cheek at the way she looks at Julian, the flicker of interest clear in her pale blue eyes. I know there's no way Julian would go there, even if she does seem like a logical choice. She would strengthen his relationship to Lev and their arms deal, and publicly she was a rich, party-girl socialite turned businesswoman. The press both loved and hated her, but she had a lifestyle that would work as a cover for many Family activities.

Alexi Volkov, her twin, grins and winks in Julian's direction as he looks him over. He's equally as beautiful, but unlike his stoic sister, his face is more relaxed, his expressions more animated. His interest is more obvious as he tries to flirt. "And if you'd like company afterwards, you have our number."

He stands with his arms crossed, dressed similarly to his sister in all black with red leather brogues. His black shirt is unbuttoned down to his navel, and I notice a silver body chain against his pale, creamy flesh, catching in the low lighting as he moves

"You work too hard Mr. Asaro, we can help you relax," he purrs as he pulls out a joint and lights it up. The sweet, sickly cloying smell quickly fills the space and for a moment no one says anything.

Taking a few steps forward I ignore Creed's whispered 'Ohhhh shit', and I fist my hand through the Russian twinks' hair, pulling him down until his eyeline is the same as mine. "I don't normally do this... but do you know who I am?"

"*Nyet,* but I know you are *bezumnyy*, little woman,"

225

he whines, trying to twist away. His large hands slap at mine, but I'm determined once I latch on. "Let go!"

Out of the corner of my eye, I see his sister step forward, but Julian raises a hand to stop her. "I'm sorry, I haven't formally introduced you. This is Rosie, Queen of Hearts."

"The Queen of Hearts?" The ice princess stands and stares at me, tilting her head from left to right in confusion and I knew I should have worn something other than a green rockabilly dress with matching heels, but I'd wanted Daniel to shit himself when he saw me alive and well, looking incredible. However, my outfit didn't exactly give off killer vibes, unless you knew who I was.

Alexi shrieks, trying to get out of my hold even harder now. "The one who eats the hearts every year?"

"I DO NOT—" I yank harder, shaking his head, ignoring Creed's howling laughter at this point. "—EAT HEARTS."

"No, she posts them lovingly to Julian," Creed unhelpfully chimes in.

Holding his hands up in defeat, Alexi goes still. "Okay, okay!"

Finally, I let go of his precious white hair, and moved back towards Julian, enjoying the way his arm sneaks around my waist and his hand rests on my hip possessively.

With a firm push, Anoushka shoves her brother towards the door. "I apologize for my brother's overtures. We'll be leaving now."

Julian nods at them and they go, muttering to one another furiously in Russian and they do. Just before they're out of sight, Anoushka slaps her hand over her brother's mouth, hissing something and glancing back at us with an uneasy smile. Moments later she yelps, as he's apparently bitten her.

"That was fun," Creed says, grinning like an idiot.

"They are chaotic, how do they manage to keep their personal and public lives separate? I'm amazed they haven't been uncovered yet." With crazy energy like theirs, it was easy to make a mistake, to slip up. Once that happened, it was game over and you'd end up in Kenfig Correctional, or if you were really unlucky, Ogmore Grange Penitentiary.

Julian puts down the duffle bag he brought with him and crouches down to unzip it. "They have a lot of money, many connections and they entertain Newtown. People in this city are charmed by them, they love reading Oliver Staddon's scathing articles and they love seeing pictures of them getting in trouble. As long as they keep that up, who will believe they're actually quite bloodthirsty and ruthless?"

He hands me my stiletto blade and garter, which I quickly slip on. Then he hands me my small handgun, which I tuck into a hidden pocket inside the skirt of my dress.

"And are they bloodthirsty and ruthless?" I ask as I re-adjust my petticoat so that my dress sits right and doesn't show any bulges where my weapons are hidden.

"Some of the best."

Creed rummages around in the bag, loads his gun and slides it into a shoulder holster I didn't even notice he was wearing. "I've never seen someone take so much pleasure in skinning a man until I'd met Anoushka Volkov."

He takes a hunting knife out of the bag, thinks better of it and puts it back before choosing a smaller blade that he tucked into the back of his trousers.

"And the brother?" I ask, through gritted teeth.

Julian laughs and gives me a pointed look. "He's a sadist. I thought you knew this, since you said he liked it rough."

Shrugging I watch as he too hides a gun on his person, even though I know he won't use it unless he has to. "I've never had sex with him, I just know someone who did."

"Are we ready?" Creed asks, closing the duffle bag and slinging it over his shoulder.

Julian grins. "As we'll ever be."

I look between the two of them, grinning. "Is this where we do some weird three musketeer chant or something?"

It was strange being here with Julian and Creed, but it also wasn't as strange as it should have been. Some part of it felt right, like we were some sort of fucked up, bad-ass team of avengers out to conquer the evil lurking in the shadows. Except, to some, we were the evil in the shadows.

"Three mafia-teers?" Creed suggests with a shrug as he unlocks the door in front of us with the keys Anoushka gave him.

"Hmmm. I like it." I glance over at Julian, whose mouth is set in a straight line as he looks between the two of us like we'd lost our damn minds.

"No. Now open the damn door," he grumbles.

Chapter Seventeen

Julian

S tepping into the room, there's nothing inside except us, two occupied chairs and a single, low hanging light with a flickering bulb. The two people tied up before us have bags of their heads and earmuff on, sensory deprivation, fuck the Volkov's were cruel. Effective, but cruel.

As agreed, Rosie and I stay back, against the far wall, hidden in the shadows as we let Eli do the work. He approached the person on the left, removing the muffs and tearing the bag from their head. Rosie stiffens beside me, obviously recognizing the person sat before us with the defiant eyes.

Elijah rips the tape off their mouth, leaving an angry red mark. "What've we got here? A pretty boy?"

They were wearing a blue corset, with intricate gold dragon embroidery and a pair of trousers that laced up the sides. Their long hair was messy thanks to the bag, but it was clearly partially braided, and threaded with gold hoops and beads.

Spitting, they hissed, "My pronouns are they/them asshole."

"Your what are what?" Eli stands for a moment, perplexed. That's when it dawns on me that we didn't actually have anyone, in my office or in The Family, who openly identified as non-binary. Hell, we didn't have women as Captains either and in 2022, that shit needed to change.

The young person wriggles against the bindings before glaring at Eli. "You aren't that ignorant, don't pretend otherwise."

Eli grabs his knife from his waistband and flips it open, running the blade down the traitor's cheek. "What do pronouns matter when we all end up nothing but skeletons in the ground anyway, hmmm?"

It's all part of the intimidation, as Eli tries to crack the obstinate attitude the person before him is displaying. Their jaw is set, their shoulders set back and their mouth is pulled into a tight straight line, all indicators that they won't be easy to break unless the right pressure is applied.

"I'm not dead yet, so it's they/them or I won't answer your questions." They huff, trying the ropes one again. "Or you may call me Cato."

"That's not how interrogation works," Eli snorts, watching his knife cut into the stranger's cheek as they struggle against the restraints.

"You don't scare me," they say, breathing erratically. "I grew up in East Point where my own father pimped me out and then sold me to his drug dealer to pay his debts. Physical pain is nothing."

I turn to look at Rosie, taking note of the way her jaw has clenched and her arms are crossed firmly over her chest, as if she were restraining herself from interfering. She didn't just know this person, she cared about them. The Queen of Hearts finally had a weak spot, and it wasn't me. For some reason, that stung more than it should have.

"The Volkov's tell us you've been spying on The Family for The Cartel, Cato." Eli grabs Cato's hair and pulls his head back hard. "Is it true?"

They look up at Eli, face blank as they reply. "Yes."

"Why? What did they offer you?"

"Money."

"What did you tell them?"

"Nothing they didn't already know." Their voice is flat, monotone and there's something unsatisfactory about their answers. Why give in so easily? Why the lack of emotion? There was no fear, no remorse, no begging, not like we usually saw with these types of interrogation.

"You're a useless mole then?" Eli goads, poking them with his knife again, this time using the handle. They don't even flinch.

"No." Another dull answer.

Eli groans, and runs a hand over his face. "You have to give us more than that Cato, or I'm going to have to cut up that pretty face of yours."

He sounds reluctant, and I'm impressed. I almost believe him. However, I know it's just a part of the interrogation, it's how Eli works and it really is something compelling to watch. Beside me, Rosie swallows. Could she handle it if we had to hurt Cato? Because if they didn't give us something, and soon, that's what would happen.

Suddenly they glare at Eli and spit again, this time in Eli's face. "I don't have to give you shit! You assholes killed Rosie, she was going to fix everything. She was going to make sure we were heard. And your fuckhead of a boss murdered her."

Eli raises a brow as he wipes the spittle from his cheek. "Rosalyn Gambino?"

Cato inhales shakily. "I thought...I really thought she was going to win. I was gathering information on The Cartel for her, making myself useful, ready for when she needed it."

Eli says nothing, standing back with his arms crossed, tapping his knife against his arm restlessly as we all watch the person before us burst into angry tears.

"But you fuckers killed her. You destroyed her life, took everything from her and then murdered her." They sob, face turning red as they struggle to breathe, shout and cry all at the same time. "This is how you treat people in The Family, and you don't even see it— too busy drinking champagne in your fucking mansions while the rest of us get trodden on."

These were my people, the ones I was supposed to protect and I was doing a poor job of it, instead focusing my attention keeping the old traditional men happy. That was how Rosie had won support, by targeting the people I overlooked every day. She looks at me, her eyebrow raised in question and when I nod my head, she rushes to Cato, getting on her knees before them.

Stroking their face, as Eli cuts their bindings, she

soothingly says, "Cato, calm down."

"Ro?" They sob harder, their whole body shaking before falling to the floor with her and pulling her into a hug.

"Heyyyy baby, it's me. Shhhhhh. Not dead, look, all in one piece." She comforts them, rocking them gently.

Sitting back, Cato glares at her. "Where the FUCK have you been? They said..."

"I know, I know," Rosie replies, cutting them off, but I notice she doesn't explain. What would she say? I've been holed up in a mansion, getting naked with Julian Asaro, the guy I hate and baking cakes? Unlikely.

"Cato, you need to tell me what you learned about The Cartel. It's really important," she requests softly, taking their face between her hands.

They swallow, sniffling as they wipe away the remainder of their tears. The shock has seemingly worn off now. "Some guy from the Six Suns Chinese crime syndicate is backing them."

I exchanged a look with Eli, whose expression seems to mirror my thoughts. We hadn't been expecting international support for The Cartel, they were just a bunch of upstarts looking to increase their territory for fuck's sake. They hadn't been around long enough and certainly weren't sophisticated enough to have any sway internationally.

"That's not possible..." Rosie remarks firmly as she gets to her feet and offers Cato a helping hand.

"Why?" Eli asks, narrowing his eyes at Rosie. There were always more secrets, more tricks to uncover with her. She was like that damn handkerchief joke the clowns at the circus used, and even though I pulled and I pulled, I doubt I'd ever reach the end with her.

"The Six Suns is run by a woman," she clarifies, looking at both Eli and me like we were idiots for not knowing that. It wasn't like organized crime groups across the world had yearly symposiums or a group chat. We were criminals for fuck's sake.

"Well, then there's been a change in leadership or something," I reply flippantly, irritated that she seemed, once again, to know more than I did. Maybe she was better suited for this role than I was? Maybe I'd been fooling myself all along thinking that I could make this Family stronger, when really, I was clueless and focusing on the wrong things.

"No, I spoke with Kiaria last week." She shakes her head. "It's not them. They aren't supporting The Cartel."

"Why would you be speaking to the Six Suns?" Eli

demands, and I can see the wheels turning inside his head and he thinks the same as I do. Was this how she was going to take me down?

"Because they have an opiate route that I think will benefit Newtown."

"You want to bring more drugs into the city?" Eli asks incredulously, as he pulls out his phone and calls one of his men in here.

"You think you can't get them already? No, I want to bring more regulated drugs in. Control the source and the flow, if you will." She laughs and rolls her eyes, sharing a 'can you believe this guy?' type of look with Cato. Turning to me, she gently says, "It was inspired by White Rabbit, but it's called Mad Hatter."

She was inspired by White Rabbit? By the way I was pushing WunderLnd Corporation forward? That was new. I mean, she'd admired my body, worshipped my cock and adored my house. But when it came to The Family and how I oversaw everything, she always had criticism, things she would do differently, better.

"We'll continue this discussion later," I reply, placing a kiss on the back of her hand, ignoring the way Cato's eyes almost bugged out of their head. "We still have another guest to question."

We all turn and look at the second figure tied to the chair. Daniel.

Chapter Eighteen
Rosie

My heart thuds loudly in my chest as Creed's man takes Cato away for further questioning, less hands-on questioning where they won't be harmed. I know I can trust Julian when he promises me that Cato will be safe, but still, seeing them tied to the chair, their cheek bleeding as they cried over me...that wasn't something I would forget any time soon.

I knew Jay would have a million questions for me later, he'd want to know how I knew Cato which would prompt a conversation about what I did when I ran away at eighteen and I wasn't quite ready to delve into that yet. I didn't know what was going to happen next, and to share those parts of myself was almost like a defeat in itself.

While we were interviewing Cato, Julian had received footage from a security camera a few blocks outside of the Church Quarter that put Daniel at the scene of the fire that morning. He was walking alone down the street, and the stills were grainy but it was clearly him. There were a few others around, but none of them were immediately recognizable, so Jay was having Creed's security team analyze the images to see if we could discover his accomplices. There was no doubt any longer, Daniel had played us both. But why?

Julian gives me a warning look, as we step back into the shadows. He'd told me not to kill Daniel, that it was his choice and his responsibility. Didn't he realize that he didn't have to make every single decision alone? A family was a unit. They should share some of those burdens too.

Creed gives us both a nod, to indicate that he's about to remove the earmuffs. Next he rips away the bag, then he roughly peels away the tape. Remind me to ask the Volkov's to wrap my Christmas presents for me this year, they were pretty fucking thorough.

Daniel squints as his eyes adjust to the low lighting, looking around anxiously as he begins to tremble.

"Elijah? I don't understand...I don't know why I'm here?"

Creed gets in close to his face and snarls, "So you don't know anything about the church?"

This interrogation is already so much different. There's a haze of rage in the room, pulsing, and swirling around us. We already know he's guilty. We just need him to confirm it.

Daniel flinches and I can feel Jay tense up beside me. It's hard seeing someone you trusted, someone you thought had your back, like this. Julian's the type of man who takes on someone else's failings, he's too responsible to be any other way and so I know that he's standing beside me, cursing himself for not doing better, for not seeing it sooner.

"That was Rosalyn Gambino," Daniel whimpers pathetically, trying to place the blame on me. He doesn't realize that we already know. A few crocodile tears fall down his cheeks as he shakes his head furiously. "How could you think it was me?"

Looking at him now, in this light, there's something familiar about his face. Without the glasses dwarfing him, his features are more defined, more recognizable. The cheekbones, the nose...if I'm right, I might know who helped him play us both.

"Liar," Creed says calmly. It appears he isn't going

for the screaming, loud tactics he used on me, nor the openly threatening ones he used on Cato. Instead, he's unnerving Daniel, getting under his skin differently as he begins to circle around the shaking man with steady footsteps. It was fascinating seeing Creed like this, and I'll admit he deserves more credit that I previously gave him. He may be a bottomless pit of a man with no manners, but he's also a chameleon, adapting himself to what's required of him.

Daniel sniffles and sobs, bringing my focus back on him. How can he be so spineless? Is it all an act? There's something off about him and it's making my skin tingle. I shift, moving so that I'm directly in front of him, even though he can't see me. He looks scared, his body is quivering and trembling, but there's a gleam in his eyes I don't like. Every time Creed passes behind him, there's a tiny change on his face and a slight hand movement. Blink and you'd miss it.

Jay comes up next to me in the darkness, that saltwater crisp smell that seems to linger around him enveloping me as his hand rests on the base of my spine. I can barely make him out in the shadows, but I think he tilts his head at me as the air changes around us. Sliding his hand into mine, we watch and wait.

When Creed is behind Daniel, I shake Jay's hand. I do it again on the next lap, and I can feel him straighten up beside me. He understands what I'm showing him.

"I swear, it was that bitch! The fucking Queen of Hearts!" He sounds sincere. Honest. But there it is again, his little tells. "I had nothing to do with it! She must have tried to frame me before you killed her."

Julian steps forward and Daniel's eyes widen before he starts begging again. Big heaving, tearless sobs. "Julian, I thought...I thought we were friends!"

Staring down at him as though he were nothing more than dirt on his shoe, Julian intones, "So did I. Funny that."

Daniel forces out more fake tears, trembling and becoming a snotty mess as he tries to curl up on himself, make himself appear smaller, more harmless.

"Stop pretending to be pathetic," Julian drawls, sounding bored. "Your fingers twitch every time your mask falls."

Daniel freezes and blinks for a moment, a confused expression on his blotchy face.

"A traitor should really work on their tells, Danny boy," Creed says as he punches him, and I can hear the sound of flesh meeting bone as he crunches against Daniel's jaw.

"Julian, you have to listen...she made me do it."

He's changing tact, interesting. "She was blackmailing me."

The sobs have stopped. His self-preservation is kicking in a little sooner than I anticipated as he tries to mitigate his involvement since the denials aren't working. He's already established that Julian knows he's lying and now his only way out is to diminish his role and his responsibility for the situation, it's clever. However, it's not clever enough.

"Rosalyn?" Jay says and it sends a shiver down my spine. Watching him work is like watching art. He's so calm, so collected as he lures Daniel into a trap. He's the smoothness to my rough and it's addicting. I love how out here in the real world, he's this responsible pillar of the community and head of The Family, and yet at home in our little bubble, he's wild. Unrestrained. Untamable. I get to see a side to him that no one else does and that sets my skin on fire.

Daniel practically bounces with excitement; he thinks Julian believes him and I have to cover my mouth to stifle the noise that escapes me. What a little fool.

"Yes! She made me set up that dinner," Daniel whined. I shrug to myself, that one was technically true and I watch as his fingers stay still. He carries on rambling. "She forced me to help her with the church, but I was going to tell you."

Lie.

I don't even need to say anything, Julian has already seen the fingers dance and we all catch the moment Daniel realizes. His eyes widen and he flinches before wriggling against his bindings in some sort of mad hope that they'll just unravel and fall at his feet.

Julian nods and without warning, Creed breaks the offending digits. The snapping noise fills the room as Daniel cries out in pain. His fingers look disgusting, bent at odd angles, and unmoving as he breaks out in a sweat, his skin turning a waxy grey color.

It doesn't last long though, it's like a switch has been flicked inside him as he glares at Julian, hate and anger clear in his eyes. Gone is the meek assistant and in his place sits a twisted, jealous monster.

"You're weak," Daniel spits, his face twisted into a mask of rage. "Making your lackeys do your dirty work."

Jay brushes off some imaginary lint from his shirt. "I don't waste time and energy on scum like you. You should know that by now Daniel."

Daniel tilts back his head and laughs. It's so forced that it's almost comical in itself. "You always were afraid of her. And we used that. We exploited your fears and your hatred. We'll keep chipping away at you Julian until you crumble because you haven't got the balls to do anything about it."

Julian raises a brow, unimpressed. "I'm afraid of Rosalyn Gambino?"

I can tell by the look on his face he was thinking the same thing as me. He wasn't afraid of me last night when he'd eaten me out like a starving man. Or when he fucked me up against the shower glass. Or when I rode him until we both came this morning?

"Petrified," Daniel sneers. "She makes you quake in your posh Italian shoes."

I bite back another laugh, I make him come while he's wearing his posh Italian shoes, does that count? Daniel really is clueless about our twisted dynamic and how we work.

"There's a difference between fear and respect." Jay leans in. "Now tell me, who set the fire? Whose idea was it to murder innocent people?"

"You won't get anything from me. I'm not afraid of you." Daniel stares straight ahead, clearly mentally preparing himself for whatever was coming next.

Julian paces back and forth in front of him for a moment before asking, "Are you afraid of the Queen of Hearts?"

"Pfft, you'd have to be stupid not to be." *Smart boy.* "Why do you think we wanted you to take care of her first?"

"Hmmm." Julian steps back and holds out a hand to me. "Rosie? Want to come and play?"

"I've been waiting for you to ask," I purr as I step forward, reveling in the way Daniel's jaw drops as I emerge from the shadows like some motherfucking nightmare.

"No...you killed her," he stammers. "She's supposed to be dead."

"Sorry, sweetie." I lean down and stroke his face. "Still very much alive, and don't worry—once I've taken care of you, Mommy is next."

"You know who his accomplice is?" Creed asks as he watches us carefully.

Taking my finger, I run it along Daniel's profile, down his forehead and following his nose, over his lips and then his chin. He has a prominent, pointed nose that I've seen before and I can't believe I never realized it, especially since she was the one to introduce us.

"Valentina Bruno. Am I right?" I ask, thinking about the elderly woman who'd sat at my table and spouted about the old ways. I move away, mentally cursing myself for not seeing her danger sooner. I knew she was unhappy with my direction; I knew she was restless but I didn't think she'd plot to have me killed by my enemy.

"Antonio's wife," Creed murmurs. "But they don't have children?"

"They don't," Jay explains, "but there was a rumor that she did before they married." It was one of those secrets that had practically become an urban legend amongst The Family. Everyone knew about it, but we never really knew if it was really true.

"The woman in the nursing home?" Creed demands as he grabs Daniel's shirt.

"She's my aunt." His mouth twists into a cruel grin as Creed shoves him away in disgust before moving away. I can see Creed's anger building, so like me, he's stepped back to collect himself. We're planners, thinkers, we anticipate the next move and to do that we need space and to stay calm. Daniel was too keyed up, and not afraid enough. He was planning something.

Julian begins pacing again as he talks, "So you plotted with your birth mother to bring us both down and what? Rule instead? Take us back to the 'old ways'? Are you delusional?"

Quick as a flash Daniel lunges at Julian with a small pocket knife clenched in his fist, murder clear in his eyes but he never gets to lay a finger on him. Before he can make contact, Creed jabs him in the throat, winding him. When he steps back, sputtering and trying to swallow in big breaths, I sneak behind him with my newly returned stiletto blade and cut his hamstrings. He drops to the floor with a thud like a bloody sack of potatoes.

"How did the Volkov's leave him with a pocketknife? Sloppy," I say as I nudge a wailing Daniel with my toe.

Jay looks at us, and frowns. "I could have handled that myself."

"Did you know he was going to do that?" Creed asks, as he kicks Daniel's writhing, moaning body. The cries and groans grow, the noise going through me and I roll my eyes.

"No. Did you?"

"Yes," we say in unison. Julian was still too trusting, too hesitating, too busy wanting to do the right thing that sometimes, he ended up putting himself in danger. I mean, look how many times I could have killed him already.

"He had too much anger to sit still for long, we just gave him an opportunity," I explain as I crouch down, grab his hair and pull his head up. Sliding my stiletto blade into his ear, I don't stop until the hilt meets resistance. He goes limp almost instantly. "I'm sorry, but I needed to hurry this up. His moaning was annoying and I have a beef joint at home."

Julian runs a hand through his hair and gives me a wry smile. "Why do I feel like I've been played?"

We hadn't deliberately tricked Julian, but when he'd spoken earlier that day about needing to be the one who chose to kill Daniel, Creed and I had looked at one another and we had just known what needed to be done.

"Would you have let us hurt him otherwise?" Creed asks as he hands me a cloth to wipe my blade on.

Rubbing his chin, Jay admits, "I was thinking about it."

"Exactly." For Julian, violence was always a last resort instead of a necessary evil. This case definitely warranted some extra brutality. We needed to put an end to the restless whispers.

"We didn't play you. We reacted and we eliminated the problem," Creed justified but we both knew that either way, Daniel was never going to be coming out of this room. He was a danger to Julian and neither Creed or I could take that risk.

Creed turns Daniel over with his foot and hands me a serrated hunting knife from the bag he brought with him. I take it with a grin, loving that I didn't even have to ask. Maybe the three mafia-teers could be a thing after all.

I shrug as I start unbuttoning Daniel's shirt. "Well, half of the problem, but Valentina is next."

Julian crouches down beside me as I line up the blade. "Rosie, what are you doing?"

Plunging it into the dead man's chest I whisper, "Sending a message."

Chapter Nineteen
Julian

"I can't believe she just did that," I say back in my home office as Eli sits and raises a brow at me. I knew Daniel had to be punished, and it's not that I was weak but I didn't want violence to be at the center of everything.

"Really?" he scoffs. "She sends you a box of hearts every year..."

It was one thing seeing the box with a heart in it, which I'd only actually seen the first time, and after that my assistant or Elijah had dealt with it. It was an entirely different thing to watch her carve it out of his chest, leaving an empty, bloody, pulp cavity. Then she'd wrapped it up in Saran wrap and held on to it

ALICE LA ROUX

the entire car journey home. It was currently sitting in a Tupperware tub in my fridge. There was a human heart in my fridge.

"I just never thought I'd actually witness her do that," I admit as I loosen my tie and pour us both a glass of whiskey. It had been a long evening. "It was like a damn biology lesson."

Eli chuckles. "I thought she was more like a butcher, she doesn't have enough finesse to be a surgeon."

I wholeheartedly agreed with that statement as I glanced down at my dirty shirt. I don't know what possessed me to wear one of my suits this evening, because now there were blood splatters on it from where Rosie had brushed against me in the car afterwards. While she was cradling Daniel's heart. Like a madwoman.

Shrugging Eli points out, "It's her 'thing'. Besides, it's visually terrifying. It sends out the right message."

"And that is?"

"Don't fuck with me. Except she's sending it from both of you now." He was right. She used a serrated hunting knife for maximum mess too, they weren't clean cuts. They were jagged and bloody, each one a warning. A terrifying, visceral warning that sent

252

shivers down my spine. But was it actually from both of us?

"What does that mean?" Was she putting aside her plans to de-throne me? Did she no longer want to kill me or was it still my fate to end up like Daniel? A shiver runs through me as I picture myself in his place.

"You're the one fucking the enemy, you tell me?" Elijah's mouth tightens as he crosses his arms. His face is serious and I know he's wondering the same thing as me: was Rosalyn Gambino still my number one threat? And if so, how did we deal with it?

"Right." I nod. We'd moved past wanting to destroy each other surely, not that I had even wanted that to begin with.

Standing and stretching, Eli gives me a look. "Maybe you need to have a discussion with her."

Yes. Maybe I do. I don't know why my brain seems to falter when it comes to her. It's like all my logical thoughts hide from her, afraid of her dark side. "Where is she?"

He shrugs. "Getting cleaned up, I guess. Go and check on her, I'll check on the dinner."

There it was again, that oddly domestic feeling. Almost like I had a home, and not just a house, and it was filled with family. Actual family, and not The Family or people who pretended to support me. I wanted to cling to this for a little longer because I wasn't ready for it to end just yet.

I smile. "You're staying for food then?"

He snorts and points towards the kitchen. "Can you smell that? Of course, I'm staying. That woman missed her calling in life."

I tilt my head, thinking about what I'd seen of Rosie Gambino this week. She'd dominated my house, been submissive in my bedroom and handled shit like a professional when I'd been faced with a threat. She's been born and raised to rule. They'd tried to break her, and she'd come back stronger. This was a role she was designed for.

"I don't know, I think she's pretty perfect as the Queen of Hearts."

I knock softly on the bathroom door before letting myself in. She's standing in fresh underwear that I bought her, the bloody clothes already bagged and on the floor by her feet as she scrubs her hands and nails in the sink.

I watch the pink water swirling down the plughole as she smiles at me in the mirror. I want to freeze this moment because she looks perfect, her cheeks flushed, blonde hair tousled, a glint in her eye, and the blood under her nails isn't even an issue because I see her for who she is. She's a killer Queen and power radiates from her. It's mesmerizing.

"So, I'm guessing you didn't come here just to watch?" she teases, turning and pulling me in for a kiss. She even tastes good, and I deepen the embrace trying to burn this memory into my brain. I want more. Always more. Why did poison have to taste so sweet?

I bury my face into her neck for a few moments, inhaling that dark cherry smell, tinged with blood and it's intoxicating.

We break apart, breathless but still wrapped up in one another and it takes me a moment to realize that she's still waiting for a response to her question.

"Huh?"

Her mouth lifts into a half-smile. "You look serious again, something you want to say?"

Oh. That's why I was here. I wanted to see where I stood, what this meant to both of us. If it meant anything at all to her. I wasn't ready to let her go yet, I hadn't had nearly enough of her. If I didn't know better, I'd think I was becoming obsessed with Rosie Gambino.

I tuck a strand of hair behind her ear. "Once we

255

deal with Valentina, the stupid little coup of theirs will be crushed. But what about you?"

She frowns, taking a step back and I want to run my thumb over her forehead and smooth out the creases, as she asks, "Me?"

"Your little rebellion?" I say with a nod, my voice solemn.

Rosie shrugs nonchalantly, avoiding my gaze. "What about it?"

I lean against the wall with my arms crossed. "What happens next?"

"We go back to before. This was just . . ." She talks with her hands, waving them as if she could conjure the right word.

When that doesn't happen, I supply it for her. "A game?"

She looks annoyed, almost insulted. "No. But this can't happen Jay. There is too much between us."

"Rosie..." I grind my teeth, I don't know why I'm getting angry; I knew it would be like this. I knew that before it even got this far. Rosie's anger was so deeply ingrained, and dear old Daddy never taught forgiveness, only hate, power and revenge.

It strikes me that we're complete opposites, my childhood was nothing but pain and hate and yet forgiveness is always my first choice. Vincent may have loved his daughter, but he was a fucking idiot for warping her into a single-minded weapon, where moving on is the last option after death.

"Your father killed my parents," she reminds me with a hiss as she tries to turn away. "You helped. Do you want me to forget that?"

I exhale sharply, frustrated at her words. Even after all this time, did she not understand what I was trying to do that night? I was twenty-two, with no influence and no power to stop anything, so I did the only thing I could.

"I didn't help him! I tried to help you," I growl, grabbing her arm and forcing her to face me.

"Help me?" She scoffs. "I could have saved them; I could have fought your father. Helped them escape. Something. *Anything*."

"No." I shake my head. "That night was inevitable. I just tried to protect you from seeing it."

She had been a clueless girl that night, completely oblivious to The Family and how it really worked. Vincent had kept her separate and trained her, but he never actually prepared her for the realities. Great, so she could kill someone, but could she navigate the political aspects? The backstabbing? The betrayals? Not everything required brute force. What he'd done was essentially build himself a protector, the ultimate subservient bodyguard, only he'd gotten himself killed before he could climb any higher up the hierarchy.

"I can't accept that," she shouts, hands balled into fists as her eyes begin to fill with tears. It's like a tightening in my chest as I see her hurt, I understand her loss. She loved them and she lost everything, my father had ensured it. However, that didn't change the fact that there was more than just one side to that night.

I try to explain carefully, but I know it's no use. "Your father was challenging Frank, stealing money from the businesses and trying to turn others against The Family. He was a traitor, Rosalyn. You know what happens to traitors, you've just done it yourself." I reach out to touch her shoulder but she shrugs me away.

"No, he wasn't...he wouldn't." She steps back away from me. She's bringing that iron wall down between us and I wish she could see that I never wanted to hurt her. I never meant to cause her more sadness.

I capture her hand in mine, trying to soothe her. "He was. They found all the ledgers and paperwork to prove it."

"I can't do this Julian," she whispers as she pulls herself free.

Pushing on, I carry on telling her what I know, what I'd learned over the years. "Your mother had an affair when you were eight, we think you might have a sibling somewhere. Your father wasn't an easy man, Rosie and your parents weren't as perfect as you think they were."

I know my words sting. I can see her flinch but I don't want any more secrets or misunderstandings between us. That night my only aim was to shield her from seeing her parents as traitors, and save her from watching them be punished for it.

"How do you feel?" I press, trying to reach her behind the barriers she was putting up so fast I barely had any hope of getting through.

Wrapping her arms around herself, she murmurs, "Confused. Sad. Angry."

"Stay with me. Be mine." It's like I've used the wrong choice of words as I see her shut off completely. Her eyes go flat and her mouth pulls into a straight line.

Pushing back her shoulders, she drawls, "I won't be your pet, Julian. It's been nice, baking and pretending that I'm some pretty little housewife. But that's not me."

I make a sound of protest but she raises her hand

to silence me. Rosalyn Gambino is not done putting me in my place just yet.

"Tonight, I acted the same as your Left Hand. I am not one of your Captains or one of your soldiers. And I won't be relegated to that role." She looks back in the mirror, running a hand through her hair and fixing her make-up.

"That's not what you are," I grind out, frustrated that she's refusing to see what's right in front of her face. The potential we have together is incredible. The chemistry is off the charts. Doesn't she feel this too?

She looks over her shoulder at me with an eyebrow raised. "Really? Because I know how everyone else will see it. Look, there's Julian, isn't it incredible how he tamed that little bitch and brought her under his thumb."

"Rosie..." I grab her wrist, but she slaps me away. I reach out and try to get hold of her again, but this time she twists my arm and slams my face against the mirror, cracking the glass.

"I think you've forgotten who I am," she sighs before letting go and turning her back on me. "It's time for me to leave."

Chapter Twenty
Rosie

I can't listen to his words. My parents, traitors, affairs, secret siblings, stealing. He doesn't know what he's talking about. I don't stop in the bedroom to grab anything as I head downstairs because everything I have here, he bought anyway.

I just need to get out of this house and away from Julian. I need to put some space between us and think about my next move. Why did he have to make things so complicated? Why couldn't we just go back to how things were before? Elijah's eyes almost pop out of his head when I stride towards the door in nothing but my underwear.

"Urm...Rosalyn?" he calls, coming out of the kitchen.

"Yeah?"

He motions to my state of undress. "You might want to grab a coat?"

"Oh." I was so angry and confused I hadn't really thought about how I was about to walk out into the suburbs in nothing but some fancy lingerie. "Eli, the beef is done. There's some mashed potatoes and gravy in the fridge, it just needs to be heated up."

"Oh shit, Daniel's heart. Can you grab it for me please?" I ask, ignoring the footsteps I can hear coming from upstairs.

Creed darts into the kitchen and quickly returns, handing me the Tupperware box, frowning. "Aren't you staying?"

I inhale and exhale slowly before answering, trying to keep it together. Trying to not let my heart shatter even though I knew it would inevitably end this way. There was no future for me here, and I refused to be someone's lackey. I didn't care how big his dick was or how he smelt like a day at the beach or how he seemed to be obsessed with my banana muffins.

"No, I'm done here. Oh, and by the way...I think I'm currently winning," I say, lifting the box with

Daniel's heart. "This puts the score at 1- 0 in my favor Creed."

"I don't think joint effort kills should count." He scoffs, shaking his head as he stands in the doorway watching me carefully.

"Ahhhh, but I'm a liar and a cheat, so I'll be claiming this one."

He throws his hands up in defeat. "Fine, but I won't go easy on you next time."

We stare at each other for a moment in silence, the three mafia-teers over before they had even begun and a new unease creeping into everything.

Finally, I sigh and give Creed an apologetic look. "Elijah...let's not run into each other again. I don't want to kill you, okay?"

"I doubt we'll have much choice." His face is serious and I know he understands what I'm saying. The second my foot is over the threshold, this alliance, this uneasy truce we've had is dissolved. We're no longer in a detente and it's back to war. He'll be back to hunting me. One of us will have to kill the other, since it's his job to protect Julian, and mine to kill him.

"True." There was no avoiding him if I want what's rightfully mine. "I'll make it quick then."

That makes him grin, his competitive side coming

out. "Don't be so cocky, Queen of Hearts. I'm not going to go down without a fight."

I nod with a small smile, accepting that this was the world I lived in. Grabbing one of Julian's longer coats, I put it on and ignored the figure looming on the stairs. Nothing he could say would stop me now anyway.

I need room to breathe.

To think.

But to do that, I had to take care of something first.

"Did I or did I not warn you not to cross me, Valentina?" I ask as I run a knife down her cheek, the tip of the blade barely breaking the skin as it sliced down like I was cutting butter. The small trail of blood is nothing and yet she whimpers.

This is why I hate dealing with the elders in The Family. They were all mouth, ranting and raving about 'the good old days', but cut them a little and they cried. I have never personally kneecapped anyone, and that was popular amongst her generation. I could do way worse, that's all I'm getting at.

"I'm sorry, I can't hear you through the gag. Let me just...there! All better!" I sit on her dining room table and cross my legs, a bored look on my face as she sobs, tied to the chair in front of me. Her dark hair is a mess, and her designer clothes are rumpled as she almost melts into her bindings. A shade of purple has started blooming around her right eye.

Esme and Paulie have accompanied me to the Bruno residence tonight, but I have two more people positioned outside should Antonio return home from work early. Paulie had to go into hiding and has been laying low at Lola's empty apartment with me, since his loyalty was uncovered. Esme volunteered to be here, she never really liked Valentina and when she heard that it was the old bat who was responsible for St Mary's, well she wanted to be included in doling out the punishment.

"Did you get my special delivery?" I ask as her sobs slow, using the knife to carve my initials into her expensive table. I look at the RG and run my fingers through the gouges. I'd sent the heart to her this morning by special delivery, waiting until she was home alone. She'd tried to barricade herself inside this gorgeous townhouse but it was already too late. I was coming for her one way or another.

With her swollen eyes, she glares at me. I can't

decide if it was my punch earlier or all the crying that was making her look like a mess. Either way, Valentina Bruno was not looking her best right now.

"Who was it?" she whispers, afraid of my answer even though she already knows. She has to. I hope it's like an ache, a giant fucking hole in her black soul. It's the least she deserves for killing those children.

I feel my lips stretch into a slow, cruel smile. "Who do you think, Mommy dearest?"

Her body slumps as she exhales, "Daniel."

"Daniel. Traitorous, little Daniel."

She spits, "You are the traitor here, your father promised us that you would be the head of this Family but all you do is lurk in the shadows like vermin."

I nod and Esme gives her a hard slap. I feel a sense of sick satisfaction as Valentina's head whips back.

"My father died so that you could have a better future. This Family was his life," I growl, leaning in. I wanted to gut the bitch for everything she'd done, but that would be over too quickly. This punishment needed to fit the crime. It would be drawn out and it would be painful, and in the end, she would be begging for mercy that I refused to give.

She scoffs, "Pfft, his greed is what got him killed. He wanted more money, more power and everyone knows it. You're just a blind, bitter child, I never should have supported you."

I smile again, her words are just designed to hurt me. I'd refused to sully my parents' memories by digging up their transgressions. It didn't matter what they did, I knew who they were. I knew that they loved me. Valentina doesn't know shit, except the fact that she's not making it through this, and now she's trying to get under my skin. It won't work. There were children in that church. Innocents. People who hadn't chosen a side and just wanted to pray. She crossed a line, and now, I was going to make her pay for it.

Stabbing my knife into the table, I stand and boom, "Valentina Bruno, I charge you with the crime of treason against your Queen. Disloyalty, deception and pure stupidity are your offences and for that, your punishment will be fucking awful. I'll make sure of it.

She starts crying again, big, heaving, wailing noises. Like mother, like son. How had I not seen the similarities sooner? Her howls grates on me just like Daniel's did and I have to bite my tongue.

Grabbing her chin, I hiss, "And for the little trick with the church, I'll make sure your entire family pays."

I hear Esme make a surprised noise; I didn't usually punish all of the family for the acts of one, but this was an exception. Well, them and the Rossi's. Frankie's boys still owed me a blood debt. I needed to clean house and know who was on my side. I wasn't going to be disobeyed. I wasn't going to watch my back amongst my own people. I didn't roll like that.

"They had nothing to do with it!" Valentina cries, struggling against her bindings.

I laugh coldly. "When the roots are rotten, you get rid of the whole tree. You should know this by now and my patience has its limits."

I walk leisurely around her, using the same tactic Creed did to confuse and disorient her. "Daniel already tested me. He died so much quicker than he should have. It was almost painless, I mean, I did cut his hamstrings, but that's nothing really. Not in comparison to what I have planned for you."

Her howls get louder and I put the gag back into her mouth, headbutting her when she tries to bite my fingers. She slumps unconscious in her chair.

Nodding to Paulie I command, "Take her away, don't give her anything to eat or drink and be at the warehouse early tomorrow. We have some work to do."

I'd shown up at The Blue Caterpillar demanding an audience with the Volkov's, which I had been surprisingly granted. In exchange for my forgiveness over Alexi hitting on Julian, they'd kindly agreed to let me use another warehouse they had over in Port Ellesmere. I think they were both more afraid that I was there to devour their hearts than anything else, and would have agreed to anything in the moment.

I listen to Paulie drag her out to the van with one of the other men, aware that Esme has been lingering behind, waiting to say something. I'd turned up at her house two nights ago, in my underwear and Julian's coat, a mess. I explained where I'd been and she updated me on Valentina trying to convince everyone I was dead and that Julian needed to be killed.

"Are you really going to punish the whole family for her crimes?" she finally asks.

I shake my head as I sit in the chair Valentina just vacated. "Antonio Bruno was plotting against Julian anyway. Cato found evidence of it and I've just been biding my time until I could get rid of the whole toxic family."

When I'd returned to Lola's flat yesterday with Paulie and found Cato waiting for me, I'd been so relieved. That's when they told me that Valentina was a plant by Antonio, put amongst my followers to push us towards killing Julian so Antonio as Consigliere could swoop in and save The Family. Lawrence was, of course, supporting the whole thing.

Fiddling with her fingers, her voice trembles a little. "So, you're helping Julian?"

"No. Yes. Fuck." I groan as I cover my face.

She comes beside me and lays a hand on my shoulder gently. "Rosie, have you ever actually thought about why you're doing this and why you hate him?"

Sighing, I reply, "I think about it every day, Esme."

We've both lost people because of what the Asaro family did that night and how things went down. But rationally I knew that wasn't Julian. That was Felix. And Frank. And my father. He played his role in all of it too. Maybe he wasn't as perfect as I'd remembered him, grief did that. But I still couldn't fall into line under Julian. That was never going to be good enough for me.

"You've spent time with him now, do you still feel the same way?"

"I don't know..." He said he tried to protect me, to shield me but I never needed that. He did. He was the naive one who needed protection, but I couldn't make myself an underling for him. If he wasn't fit to sit on the throne then he needed to be removed.

"Is there no way to compromise?"

I groan again in response.

Chuckling, she says, "Let's make this simple: do you want to kill him?"

"No. But I will if I have to." I don't want to hurt him. I think it may actually hurt me too, but I need to put my Family first. The people who've looked after me for the last ten years deserve better.

"I really hope it doesn't come to that."

"Me too," I mumble as I wipe away the lone tear that slides down my cheek.

Chapter Twenty-One

Julian

I find myself called down to the Church Quarter, to St Mary's once again on an early Sunday morning and as I get out of the car and push my way past the crowds gathering, my stomach turns. It's chaos as people shout, desperate to know what is happening and the fire department tries to contain a small fire. The police arrive seconds after me and begin trying to move people back, cordoning off the area with tape.

"Are they...?" I squint at the scene before me, trying to take it all in. "What the fuck am I looking at?"

"The Bruno family," Elijah confirms with a sharp

nod. There's no anger in his face and for some reason that unnerves me. This is different to last time, even though the crime isn't any less brutal. In fact, it's more horrifying. More gory. What does he know that I don't?

There are four bodies, or the remains of four bodies, laid out at the bottom of what remains of the stone entry steps. The charred remains of the church sit, like black mountains just behind. The bodies hands and feet are missing and their chests are cracked wide open and appear to be oozing black liquid. I don't even need to get closer to know that I won't find their hearts in there.

"I can tell which one is Antonio, but who are the others?" Eli asks as he peers over the figures. The tall, larger framed one was definitely Antonio but the rest were all of roughly the same height and size, two were female and one male, their clothes all covered in the black liquid and blood. "Are their eyes missing?"

"It's Antonio, Valentina and then Antonio's sister and nephew," I deduce looking at the mess, resisting the urge to gag, glad I hadn't had breakfast that morning. Not that my housekeeper's pasties could compete with Rosie's. It just wasn't the same without her there, singing as she flipped pancakes over my stove. "I think so."

"I wonder if that's what's burning then. It kind of smells like meat cooking out here." He points out the small fire being extinguished near where the bodies are displayed.

"Look at the steps," I whisper, as I nudge him a little closer.

"Nasty..." he murmurs.

A shrine had been made of children's toys, photographs, white roses and candles but at the bottom of the steps lay four hearts, and it looked like they'd all been dipped in tar or something black and sticky as it spilled down the concrete. This was Rosie's apology to the victims, and her warning to anyone else who wanted to cross her. She was fucking terrifying when she wanted to be.

"We need to get to the office now. This is going to cause a shitstorm." I rub my face, a headache already building in my temples.

"I have some information you need to see before the others arrive," Eli says, his voice grim and his face serious. I nod and together we leave, trying to prepare for what comes next.

Once this madness was sorted, I needed to find Rosie and get her to talk to me. It had been four days since she'd stormed out of my house and it was driving me mad. My home was back to being lonely and cold without the craziness of her. It was throwing me off-kilter and I wasn't sure how to center myself again. I didn't care that she was the Queen of Hearts, I just wanted her to be mine.

I haven't even finished my first cup of coffee or opened the mail piled up in front of me when Lawrence storms into my boardroom with three of the other Captains, Riccardo, Tulio, Vincenzo and a few senior members of The Family. The other four Captains, Nicco, Zeno, Matteo Jr. and Carlo, enter a few moments later and I'm glad Eli had managed to get them down here so quickly. I wasn't about to let Lawrence challenge me in my own offices, on my turf without any back up from the Captains who weren't busy kissing his ass.

I can feel Eli tense behind me as Lawrence begins his tirade.

"You need to kill Rosalyn Gambino for this. Antonio Bruno was a respected member of The Family, a pillar of our community and to defile his body like that...disgusting!" He screams before slamming a hand down on the table. "You cannot let this go. You are weak and foolish to think she'll ever stop."

I am sick of being called weak.

I am sick of how this Family runs on patriarchal, macho man bullshit. Rosie wasn't uncontrollable, she was angry at a twisted system that robbed her of everything. I wanted to change The Family, but it was futile while my own Captains didn't respect me. I was tired of fighting an uphill battle while everyone looked down their noses at me, thinking they knew better.

Standing, I take one step toward him and ram my letter opener into his hand, pinning it to my table. He falls to his knees howling as blood begins to form like a lake on the wood beneath his hand.

Calmly, I grab a fistful of his hair and yank his head back. "As the head of The Family I take great offence at being called weak. Say one more word Lawrence and I'll cut out your tongue. Understand?"

He glowers at me, but nods.

"Everyone take a seat. Now," I command and they sit at my table, like meek little sheep scrambling to get into the pen. No wonder Rosie enjoyed being so bossy, it gave me a thrill to see them obeying without protest. That was the kind of respect I wanted, it was just a shame I had to shed blood to get it.

I begin walking the length of the room as I talk. "Rosalyn Gambino will not be executed. And if anyone harms a single hair on her head, I'll kill them and strip their families of the generous gifts they've been bestowed by The Family over the years."

Tulio opens his mouth as if to protest, and I turn, glaring at him as I growl, "I will take *everything*."

There are a few looks shared across the table but no one else dares to say anything. The Family has always been very liberal with how property and businesses are divided and as a result, some of these men are very rich. Money is always a powerful motivator.

I carry on, while I have their undivided attention. "This Family is broken, it's at war within itself. We're so busy focusing on this internal turf war between Rosie, I and whoever else wants to throw their hat into the ring, that the annual reports show we're neglecting our businesses. We're at risk of outsiders coming in and stealing everything from under us."

Elijah hands me some folders and I throw them down, not caring that they scatter everywhere. "There were two major threats on our territory this year. Two!"

Some of the Captains flinch and I know I'm hitting them where it hurts.

"The Cartel stopped our import of White Rabbit for a few weeks, and what were you all doing? Plotting behind my back, trying to push me to focus on

Rosalyn Gambino and listening to this fuckwit." I nod towards Lawrence, who's still pinned in place on his knees before me.

I catch Elijah's eye and he grins from the back of the room. He's enjoying this more than he should, but he's been warning me to scare my higher-ups for a while. He said it would be good for them to see what they stand to lose and why they should trust me. I'm not just a mafia man, born and bred but I'm also a businessman, a man of the law which means I know all the right loopholes to exploit.

"I'm going to be reforming this little Family of ours, and if you don't like it you can leave. I am not my father and I am not Frank. Violence isn't the only option, and if you feel like it is, then you don't belong here. Am I making myself clear?"

Silence.

Finally, someone speaks up. It's one of the Family elders, a man who goes by the name Emilio. "What about Antonio? We need justice!"

The others murmur in agreement, looking to one another for the confidence to speak against me.

I wave my hand casually over to Lawrence. "Antonio Bruno was a traitor, as is dear Lawrence here. They've both been plotting against me and if you need evidence of that, Creed will be providing you with handouts and you may ask him any further questions after this meeting."

My words are met with silence, and a few shocked faces as they begin looking towards Eli whose started giving out the pages we'd just spent an hour putting together and hastily printing. I wasn't going to waste my time verbally defending myself, not when I had more important things to do. I sit back at the head of the table and take a sip of my lukewarm coffee calmly as I let it all sink in and allow them to read the packs containing photos, screenshots, conversation transcripts and eyewitness accounts that put Antonio and Lawrence in cahoots for planning a coup and placing the blame at Rosie's feet. No one says anything and I take their lack of protest as understanding.

"As of this moment, we are starting over and we are going to make this Family stronger," I say with a smile and a few of them nod. Checking my watch, I grab my jacket and shrug it on. "Now excuse me, there's a woman who wants me dead but I'm not inclined to give her the satisfaction."

Chapter Twenty-Two

Rosie

"He did what?" The line crackles and I think maybe I've heard Esme wrong.

"He's restructuring The Family Tree, so he got rid of some of the Captains and he's replaced them with women." Her voice cuts in and out, but I heard enough to understand what she said.

"Why?" I ask as I make my way downtown. I booked a cooking class this afternoon under a fake name and was looking forward to making a walnut and coffee cake with butter icing. It was a treat to myself after dealing with the Bruno family. I hated messy kills; poison was my specialty but sometimes you needed to make a splash. I was also hoping to meet some new people, some non-Family people since Lola was still out of town and Cato was busy working as a spy for Julian now. It had been part of their punishment and a way to earn forgiveness from The Family. I was alone again.

"Apparently he wants to make The Family stronger." Esme sounds impressed and I try to ignore the pang of jealousy in my chest. I miss him. I shouldn't miss him. He wasn't mine to miss.

"Well, fuck. There go my main supporters," I laugh as I reach the building. There was no point in stressing about it right now, instead, I was going to bake away my worries. "I have to go, we'll talk later."

I climb up two flights of stairs to the culinary studio where the class takes place, except there's no one here. I frown, looking around and quickly double check the address on my phone.

"Am I in the wrong place?" I ask myself quietly.

"I paid for a private lesson," a familiar voice calls. I don't have to turn around to know it's Julian. I'd recognize that smooth timbre anywhere.

"I'm sorry, are you looking for a fight?" I say crossing my arms and glaring at him.

He holds his hands up in surrender and offers me a small smile. "No, I just want to make a cake. With you."

I've missed his smile. I've missed the way he smells. I've missed him.

Fuck.

He takes a step towards me. "Consider it a negotiation talk."

"There is no negotiating to be done between us Jay," I say firmly as I move back. If he comes too close, I don't know what I'll do. I might kill him just to end the way my chest feels like it's tightening.

He takes another step and hands me an apron from the counter. "Give me a chance, just while we make a..."

"Coffee and walnut cake," I supply. He bought out the whole class, but he didn't even know what we were making?

"While we make a coffee and walnut cake," he smiles again. "That's my favorite actually."

I look away as I whisper, "I know."

I don't miss the expression on his face as I sigh and place my bag down. "Don't get any funny ideas. I'm here for the cake."

I grab the instruction card that the tutor was supposed to run through with us and have a quick read. It looks like Julian has arranged for all the ingredients to be left out and we're going to work through it on our own.

"First we need to shell the walnuts," I say grabbing one of the small hammers and a handful of walnuts.

Julian eyes me warily. "Why aren't they already done?"

"Because this is a class where we do it from scratch," I say brandishing my hammer like Thor. I grab one of the walnuts and place it on the counter, slamming the hammer down. I can feel Jay flinch next to me as the nut shatters. "Why are you here? What do you want from me?"

"I've been trying to think of a way we can work together," he explains as he begins measuring out the butter.

I snort, bringing my hammer down again. "That's impossible, Julian. I want everything you own, it's as simple as that."

He's now pouring the sugar into a bowl on the scales. I watch him out of the corner of my eye as he meticulously checks the weight, he'd be good with positions if he was this careful with cake. "But there's a way I don't have to die for you to get it."

For a moment it feels like my heart leaps into my throat, but I swallow and shake away any stupid thoughts I have. This cannot end happily ever after; we don't get those kinds of endings.

"I highly doubt it," I say with a sigh as I place my walnut pieces into a bowl and use the electric whisk to beat the butter. "You're not just going to hand everything over to me and walk away."

"No. I'm not," he says as he slowly begins to add sugar to the butter. "I'm going to do what I should have done in the beginning and make you my Queen."

I turn the whisk off and set it to one side. "I'm sorry, I think I'm going a little deaf, what did you just say?"

He grins at me. "Be my partner. Marry me and share everything equally."

What did he just say? Has he lost his mind? I drop the egg I'm about to crack on the counter and it smashes, egg yolk running onto the floor. "And why would I agree to this?"

He winks. "Because we both know you don't want to kill me, I'm too pretty."

How can he be so flippant about what he's saying? Is it just a joke to him? Does he realize how many uproars this will cause in The Family? They won't stand for this. They can't. There's too much bad blood between my family and his for this to ever work, and yet I find myself saying, "How would this marriage work?" His grin gets wider, if that's even possible and I flick egg yolk at him.

"You're not that pretty," I grumble but it's too late, I've already shown my weakness and his hands come around my waist as he nuzzles into me. "It would work the same way most marriages work. We'd be a team in all matters. We'd fuck, fight and love each other while ruling over our Kingdom fairly." He's proposing a genuine marriage, and all without batting an eyelid. "The Family will fall into line; I'll make sure of it."

I raise a brow. "Fairly?"

"Meaning forgiveness in some circumstances..." His voice trails off and I understand what he's offering.

"And punishment in others," I finish firmly for him. He wasn't judging my methods or how I chose to handle issues, he just wanted to make sure we were on the same page and that there was a balance between the two. He was the light to my dark, the calm to my rage and it shouldn't, but it worked.

"Do I get a crown?" I tease, and find myself forgetting how to breathe as he lifts me onto the counter and wraps my legs around his waist.

Pulling me down to meet his lips for a kiss, he murmurs, "Rosie Asaro, I'm going to fuck you when you're wearing nothing but a crown."

"I feel like you have a fetish for fucking me in

kitchens." I grin at him as he quickly yanks my jumper up over my head and tosses it aside before pushing my skirt up.

"I like seeing you messy, smelling like cinnamon and cherries, good enough to eat." He kisses down my neck with each word, nibbling and biting, swirling his tongue over every dip and groove. Exploring me with his mouth like he wanted to commit me to memory.

He pulls down the soft cups of my bra, sucking my nipple into his mouth without mercy, without tenderness, only want and need as he feasts on my body. His other hand glides down my back, fingers dancing down my spine, overwhelming my senses before he pushes my hips closer to him.

Rocking gently, I grind against him. The harsh feel of the denim against my lace thong drives me insane and I groan loudly.

Julian steps back, and I pull at his jumper. "Wha— what're you doing? Why did you stop?"

"I still have some apologizing to do." He pulls his navy jumper off and places it by mine.

"That is not a reason to stop right now," I grumble as he undoes his belt buckle and undoes the button on his jeans.

"But apologies are better given down on my knees." With a devious smirk, he gets down onto the floor. "Baby, I am going to make you come and then I'm going to flip you over and fuck you hard until you're begging me to stop."

"That will never happen," I say smugly. I love it when he's rough with me. When he just takes what he wants unapologetically. That's the Jay I fell in love with.

Julian pushes my legs apart, opening me up for him without hesitation. Kissing my thighs, sucking my skin gently before lavishing it with more kisses, he moves up slowly. When his face is inches away from my pussy, he gently blows across the already sensitive flesh, making me shiver.

Using his thumbs he parts my lips and places a tender kiss on my clit, teasingly. I should have known he was only toying with me when moments later, he sucks the sensitive flesh hard, making my body spasm. His tongue worships me, repeatedly. Over and over again, while his hands move up my thighs, over my stomach, down to grab my ass. I start whining, begging for his cock inside me and that's when he's decided I've had enough taunting.

"Come on, Rosie. Come for me." His tongue flicks over my clit, unrelenting. Every suck and swirl was punishing and ruthless as he tried to pull my orgasm from me.

He slides a finger inside me, fucking me in time with the tempo from his tongue, driving me wild as my hips began to buck against his face.

"Jay, oh fuck. Jay!" I cry out, grabbing hold of his golden hair and riding his face like it was my damn job. He adds a second finger, and that sends me over the edge, my body clenching as I try to stop myself from clamping my legs shut around Julian's ears.

"We're not done yet, my love," he murmurs against my sensitive pussy, my body twitching with every word.

Lowering my legs and getting to his feet, he strips my skirt off me and turns me around, until I'm bent over the worktop, my tits squashed against the cold metal, and slightly sticky from the residual icing sugar and the egg that I'd cracked earlier.

He quickly rids himself of his shoes and jeans, kicking them aside. Grabbing my hips, I watch over my shoulder as he admires the view, hands moving over the back of my thighs, and up over my ass lovingly.

"One day, I'm going to fuck your ass too. And then I'll have owned every single part of you." There's that primal, animal instinct flaring up again. And holy hell, if I didn't get butterflies hearing him talk like that.

I flash him a saucy grin. "Mmmm, I never knew you were so filthy Jay. I think I like it."

Without warning, he slams into me, forcing a low groan from me as he fills me up in a way that only he can. Fisting a handful of my hair, he pulls me upright, my back arching against his chest as he leans down and bites on my earlobe. "We both know you love it."

His fingers dig into my tit as he fucks me, the other still knotted in my hair.

"I do," I grunt with another pump.

He thrusts hard, slamming my hips against the counter and I couldn't care less than I do right now, enjoying the bite of pain with his weight pinning me in place.

The hand in my hair shifts lower, coming around my throat the way I like it. I've never trusted anyone else enough to let them put their hands around my throat, but he was different. His thumb presses down as he fucks me, making my mind go hazy and fuzzy around the edges. I didn't often come from just penetration, but like this I could. I can feel it building, and the way he dominates every sense and every feeling has my nerves on edge waiting for release.

The other hand comes down and gives my ass a playful smack. Grabbing a bottle of olive oil from the counter, he pours it down my crack. I turn my neck to kiss him over my shoulder, our mouths clashing together as the golden oil sticks between us. The slick liquid is slightly greasy as he uses a thick finger to massage my tight hole before sliding inside. *Fuck.*

Yes.

He doesn't stop fucking me, his other hand still around my throat as he pounds into me. Jay pushes me closer and closer to the edge, my orgasm building like a storm gathering as he pushes another large finger inside me, making me feel so incredibly hot and full as he stretches me out. The double penetration of my body is the ultimate display of power and his need to own every inch of me.

Mouth by my ear, he whispers, "You are mine. My Queen. My everything."

The over stimulation drives me wild, and my thoughts are no longer coherent, just jumbled images and words as he seems to fuck all sense out of me.

Want more.

Deeper.

Harder.

So.

Fucking.

Full.

Yes.

More.

Almost.

There.

As his teeth clamp into my neck, a second orgasm is ripped from my body, leaving me a sobbing mess as I collapse against the cool stainless-steel counter.

This is what should have been mine all along.

Epilogue

Julian

"Why are we meeting in a diner?" the man before me grumbles, looking around at the 1950s themed decor with disgust. I like it, I think it's quirky, just like its owner.

I look around, taking in the empty booths. It's quiet this morning, which is perfect for what we're about to discuss. I sip on my coffee and smile at the beautiful blonde behind the counter. "Because this is where they have the best coffee and walnut cake."

He grunts, "I didn't come here for cake Julian. I want what is rightfully mine, I want that factory down by the river."

Even after six months I was still coming across the occasional shithead who thought I owed him everything. The Family was revamped, things were still in progress but now everything was shared fairly and rewards were given for hard work. It was more like a real family every passing day as we did our best to foster an inclusive sense of community within the organization but men like Carl DeLuca still just did what they pleased. And I couldn't allow that.

"The one you stole in the aftermath of the Bruno deaths, you mean?" I ask firmly, finding it ironic that those who had demanded justice for Antonio had also been the ones to squabble over his properties and businesses.

He shrugs, avoiding my gaze. "I didn't steal it; I just seized an opportunity..."

"To steal from me," I finish for him with a hard stare. "So, I've taken it back and it will be redistributed fairly."

Slamming a hand down on the table he raises his voice, "This is bullshit, fucking bullshit."

I raise my hand in an attempt to calm him, while keeping my voice level I reiterate what he has been told before. "Carl, I've given you several warnings about this and I've told you to remove your men from the property. You've been amply warned."

"Because it's mine you fucking prick!" he bellows.

"Excuse me," Rosie's soft voice calls. "This is your first warning."

"Fuck you," he screams, flipping her off before turning back to me. "This Family is fucked and you're just dragging it down! You piece of shit."

I say nothing as he stands, shouting about "Fucking autocratic bullshit."

"I wouldn't do that if I were you," I warn as Carl reaches into his jacket for his gun. His eyes are focused on one of my new bodyguards, who's sitting in the booth behind me since Eli is away investigating The Cartel for me, not realizing that he's not the threat here.

His lips twist into a snarl. "Fuck yo—"

The words die in the air as blood begins to trickle from the corner of his mouth.

"Esme, clean up on table three!" Rosie shouts as she drops Carl's body to the floor, her blade protruding from his ribcage. She may not carve out chests anymore, but that didn't mean she wasn't an expert at getting her knife right in the sweet spot.

"Cato, add the DeLuca estates to the re-distribution lists," I call over to my assistant who's been sitting at the counter, and they take out their phone to make the necessary arrangements.

"I did warn him," Rosie says sweetly as she slides onto my lap, her hands coming around my neck.

"You did," I agree as I kiss my Queen of Hearts, ignoring the body by our feet.

A few moments later Cato's phone rings, their face shifts into an expression of panic as they turn towards us.

"What's the matter?" Rosie asks as we both stand.

"It's Creed," Cato's voice trembles. "Elijah's been arrested. They're sending him to Ogmore Grange. Judge Walters signed the paperwork an hour ago."

Acknowledgments

J as always, thank you for being the domestic god you are and taking care of me while I was sick, encouraging me to rest and cheering me on while I struggled to get the words down between coughing fits. You helped keep me sane, get better and smash out the final words.

Ash, thank you for letting me use your thesis idea board as a murder board. WHERE IS DADDY VOLKOV? Who killed the Walrus?!

Annamarie, you're a star. Thank you for nagging me for this book. Firebird 2 will happen. At some point. Lizzie, thank you for helping me pull this together when we're both ill. I owe you! I wouldn't have finished this without the Filthy B**ches Sprinting group. Genuinely couldn't have done it without you! Glenna, you're a machine. I have no words.

About the Author

Alice La Roux is a dirty minded, mouthy Welsh author who likes to write strong women, the men who support them and the people who fill their lives with sarcasm, love and snacks.

She's a bookworm who reads anything: her comfort reads are dragon mpreg books and she finds dark reads palette cleansers. Ohhhhh, she's also the owner of Indie Love Wales and will be hosting a book signing in Cardiff in 2023.

Facebook: @asmadasAlice
Instagram: @alicelaroux
TikTok: @alicelaroux

Also by Alice La Roux

Firebird

Two's Company

Sinclair

Master

Addicted to Love

The Good Girl

Breeding Lilacs

Also coming in 2022

White Rabbit

Survival Games written under the name AJ Everheart

TAG

Hide & Seek

For exclusive teasers, sneak peeks and short stories, please sign up to her newsletter

Read on for an exclusive look at White Rabbit –
coming October 5th 2022!

Note: This is unedited and subject to change.

the White Rabbit

ALICE LA ROUX

Creed

I'd fucked up big time. This was not where I was supposed to be. Metal jangles around my wrists as I sit silently in the back of the transport truck. It rocks gently side to side as we head down a dirt track into the middle of nowhere. Prison. Fucking prison. How could I have been stupid enough to get caught? I was supposed to be investigating a lead The Jabberwocky sent me about some hotshot The Cartel were fawning over. Instead, I was here.

I put my head in my hands and groan softly, causing the officers either side of me to glance over suspiciously. There had to be a fucking rat amongst my men. A traitor. I was always meticulous, something my father taught me. I never left any stone unturned. Burn it all, bleach it, wipe it down, dispose of it—I did them *all* to ensure that not even a smudged partial print could be found. Rat. And when I found out who it was, I was going skin them alive. But first I had to clear my name. I was guilty of my crimes, there's no doubt about that but there's no way in hell anyone should have been able to prove it. Men like me didn't just get caught by chance. I'd been groomed for this role since I was ten. I'd spent a short stint in a Juvenile Detention Centre when I fucked up at fourteen and never looked back. My father made sure I'd learned my lesson. Idiots get caught. Incompetence and stupidity were two things he could not tolerate. He was a hard man, Augustine Creed, and I had to face some harsh truths about the world from a young age but it made me who I am today, it elevated me to The Left Hand.

We finally pull up outside Ogmore Grange prison and I can feel a chill in my bones. I'd never been here before; we always ensured that any of ours were taken care of in Kenfig Prison back in Newtown. We ran that shithole. But this, this was new territory. I needed a plan, I have enemies. Lots of them. All dying to be the one who teaches Elijah Creed, The Left Hand, a lesson. Being in The Family wasn't like the movies, those stereotypes barely scratched the surface. It was bloodier, dirtier and the risk of death was higher. Julian, my boss and close friend, ran Newtown mostly undetected and off the radar. He hid in the shadows of the city that never slept like his father and his father before him, using his wealth and his public persona like an invisibility cloak.

I was being shipped out to the suburbs, to where the authorities assumed I'd be too far out of reach to cause trouble. They were clueless. They underestimated who I was. I was The Left Hand not only because I was smart, reliable and from a mafia family but because I was also ruthless, merciless and violent. The bloodier, the better. Messed up was often a word used when people spoke of me in hushed tones and I didn't give a shit. It's one of the reasons I counted the Queen of Hearts as one of my closest friends, she understood how I worked. She appreciated the tactics I used.

We move through security and check in quickly. They call it processing but I prefer to think of it like a hotel, I won't be a guest here for long but needs must for business. We head through yet another metal gate and I get a glimpse into a community work room. A petite woman in uniform with big brown eyes and long dark hair is standing at the front delivering a workshop of some sort. She wears a smudge of blue paint on her cheek and a look of exasperation on her face. She bites her lip nervously when she sees me, and I grin. There's something about making others uncomfortable that gets me off, just a little. I like to see the fear in their eyes, their mind ticking away trying to find an escape route. I am every inch the predator. And she was all prey.

"What's that?" I ask nodding at the door as we shuffle past, my feet now shackled too.

"It's one of the workshops we deliver at Ogmore." The officer checks his watch. "I think 3pm is art with Officer Bishop."

"Art huh," I drawl, a plan already forming in my head. Officer Bishop could be a useful distraction, especially if I was going to be stuck in here for the foreseeable future.

I say nothing else as I'm stripped, searched, stamp my fingerprints on a piece of paper and assigned to a cell. It wouldn't do to cause trouble just yet, I needed to get my bearings first.

Coming October 5th 2023
Pre-order your copy on Amazon today!

Printed in Great Britain
by Amazon

42946686R00182